A HAT TRICK OF HORRID HENRY

Francesca Simon

Illustrated by Tony Ross

Orion
Children's Books

First published in Great Britain in 2007
by Orion Children's Books
a division of the Orion Publishing Group Ltd
Orion House
5 Upper St Martin's Lane
London WC2H 9EA

An Hachette Livre UK Company

5 7 9 10 8 6 4

ISBN 978 1 84255 575 0

A catalogue record for this book
is available from the British Library

Printed in Great Britain by
Clays Ltd, St Ives plc

www.orionbooks.co.uk

A HAT TRICK OF HORRID HENRY

Francesca Simon spent her childhood on the beach in California, and then went to Yale and Oxford Universities to study medieval history and literature. She now lives in London with her English husband and their son. When she is not writing books whe is doing theatre and restaurant reviews or chasing after her Tibetan Spaniel, Shanti.

Also by Francesca Simon

Horrid Henry
Horrid Henry and the Secret Club
Horrid Henry Tricks the Tooth Fairy
Horrid Henry's Nits
Horrid Henry Gets Rich Quick
Horrid Henry's Haunted House
Horrid Henry and the Mummy's Curse
Horrid Henry's Revenge
Horrid Henry and the Bogey Babysitter
Horrid Henry's Stinkbomb
Horrid Henry's Underpants
Horrid Henry Meets the Queen
Horrid Henry and the Abominable Snowman

Horrid Henry's Big Bad Book
Horrid Henry's Wicked Ways
Horrid Henry's Evil Enemies
Horrid Henry Rules the World
Horrid Henry's Joke Book
Horrid Henry's Jolly Joke Book
Horrid Henry's Mighty Joke Book

Don't Cook Cinderella
Helping Hercules

and for younger readers
Don't Be Horrid, Henry

CONTENTS

HORRID HENRY

AND THE

MEGA-MEAN TIME MACHINE

For my sister, Anne Simon,
who reminded me about
our time machine

CONTENTS

1

HORRID HENRY'S HiKE

Horrid Henry looked out of the window. AAARRRGGGHHH! It was a lovely day. The sun was shining. The birds were tweeting. The breeze was blowing. Little fluffy clouds floated by in a bright blue sky.

Rats.

Why couldn't it be raining? Or hailing? Or sleeting?

Any minute, any second, it would happen…the words he'd been dreading, the words he'd give anything not to hear, the words –

'Henry! Peter! Time to go for a walk,' called Mum.

'Yippee!' said Perfect Peter. 'I can wear my new yellow wellies!'

'NO!' screamed Horrid Henry.

Go for a walk! Go for a walk! Didn't he walk enough already? He walked to school. He walked home from school. He walked to the TV. He walked to the computer. He walked to the sweet jar *and* all the way back to the comfy black chair.

Horrid Henry walked plenty. Ugghh. The last thing he needed was more walking. More chocolate, yes. More crisps, yes. More *walking*? No way! Why oh why

couldn't his parents ever say, 'Henry! Time
to play on the computer.' Or 'Henry, stop
doing your homework this minute! Time
to turn on the TV.'

But no. For some reason his mean,
horrible parents thought he spent too
much time sitting indoors. They'd been
threatening for weeks to make him go on
a family walk. Now the dreadful moment
had come. His precious weekend was
ruined.

Horrid Henry hated nature. Horrid
Henry hated fresh air. What could be
more boring than walking up and down
streets staring at lamp posts? Or sloshing
across some stupid muddy park? Nature
smelled. Uggh! He'd much rather be
inside watching TV.

Mum stomped into the sitting room.

'Henry! Didn't you hear me calling?'

'No,' lied Henry.

'Get your wellies on, we're going,' said

3

Dad, rubbing his hands. 'What a lovely day.'

'I don't want to go for a walk,' said Henry. 'I want to watch *Rapper Zapper Zaps Terminator Gladiator.*'

'But Henry,' said Perfect Peter, 'fresh air and exercise are so good for you.'

'I don't care!' shrieked Henry.

Horrid Henry stomped downstairs and flung open the front door. He breathed in deeply, hopped on one foot, then shut the door.

'There! Done it. Fresh air *and* exercise,' snarled Henry.

'Henry, we're going,' said Mum. 'Get in the car.'

Henry's ears pricked up.

'The car?' said Henry. 'I thought we were going for a walk.'

'We are,' said Mum. 'In the countryside.'

'Hurray!' said Perfect Peter. 'A nice *long* walk.'

'NOOOO!' howled Henry. Plodding along in the boring old park was bad enough, with its mouldy leaves and dog poo and stumpy trees. But at least the park wasn't very big. But the *countryside*?

The countryside was enormous! They'd be walking for hours, days, weeks, months, till his legs wore down to stumps and his feet fell off. And the countryside was so dangerous! Horrid Henry was sure he'd be swallowed up by quicksand or trampled to death by marauding chickens.

'I live in the city!' shrieked Henry. 'I don't want to go to the country!'

'Time you got out more,' said Dad.

'But look at those clouds,' moaned Henry, pointing to a fluffy wisp. 'We'll get soaked.'

'A little water never hurt anyone,' said Mum.

Oh yeah? Wouldn't they be sorry when he died of pneumonia.

'I'm staying here and that's final!' screamed Henry.

'Henry, we're waiting,' said Mum.

'Good,' said Henry.

'*I'm* all ready, Mum,' said Peter.

'I'm going to start deducting pocket money,' said Dad. '5p, 10p, 15p, 20 – '

Horrid Henry pulled on his wellies, stomped out of the door and got in the car. He slammed the door as hard as he could. It was so unfair! Why did he never get to do what *he* wanted to do? Now he would miss the first time Rapper Zapper had ever slugged it out with Terminator

Gladiator. And all because he had to go
on a long, boring, exhausting, horrible
hike. He was so miserable he didn't even
have the energy to kick Peter.

'Can't we just walk round the block?'
moaned Henry.

'N-O spells no,' said Dad. 'We're going
for a lovely walk in the countryside and
that's that.'

Horrid Henry slumped miserably in his
seat. Boy would they be sorry when
he was gobbled up
by goats. Boo hoo,
if only we hadn't
gone on that walk
in the wilds,
Mum
would
wail.

Henry was right, we should have listened to him, Dad would sob. I miss Henry, Peter would howl. I'll never eat goat's cheese again. And now it's too late, they would shriek.

If only, thought Horrid Henry. That would serve them right.

All too soon, Mum pulled into a carpark, on the edge of a small wood.

'Wow,' said Perfect Peter. 'Look at all those lovely trees.'

'Bet there are werewolves hiding there,' muttered Henry.

'And I hope they come and eat *you*!'

'Mum!' squealed Peter. 'Henry's trying to scare me.'

'Don't be horrid, Henry,' said Mum.

Horrid Henry looked around him. There was a gate, leading to endless meadows bordered by hedgerows. A muddy path wound through the trees and across the fields. A church spire stuck up in the distance.

'Right, I've seen the countryside, let's go home,' said Henry.

Mum glared at him.

'What?' said Henry, scowling.

'Let's enjoy this lovely day,' said Dad, sighing.

'So what do we do now?' said Henry.

'Walk,' said Dad.

'Where?' said Henry.

'Just walk,' said Mum, 'and enjoy the beautiful scenery.'

Henry groaned.

'We're heading for the lake,' said Dad, striding off. 'I've brought bread and we can feed the ducks.'

'But *Rapper Zapper* starts in an hour!'

'Tough,' said Mum.

Mum, Dad, and Peter headed through the gate into the field. Horrid Henry trailed behind them walking as slowly as he could.

'Ahh, breathe the lovely fresh air,' said Mum.

'We should do this more often,' said Dad.

Henry sniffed.

The horrible smell of manure filled his nostrils.

'Ewww, smelly,' said Henry. 'Peter, couldn't you wait?'

'MUM!' shrieked Peter. 'Henry called me smelly.'

'Did not!'

'Did too!'

'Did not, smelly.'

'WAAAAAAAAA!' wailed Peter. 'Tell him to stop!'

'Don't be horrid, Henry!' screamed Mum. Her voice echoed. A dog walker passed her, and glared.

'Peter, would you rather run a mile, jump a stile, or eat a country pancake?' said Henry sweetly.

'Ooh,' said Peter. 'I love pancakes. And a

country one must be even more delicious than a city one.'

'Ha ha,' cackled Horrid Henry, sticking out his tongue. 'Fooled you. Peter wants to eat cowpats!'

'MUM!' screamed Peter.

Henry walked.

And walked.

And walked.

His legs felt heavier, and heavier, and heavier.

'This field is muddy,' moaned Henry.

'I'm bored,' groaned Henry.

'My feet hurt,' whined Henry.

'Can't we go home? We've already walked miles,' whinged Henry.

'We've been walking for ten minutes,' said Dad.

'Please can we go on walks more often,' said Perfect Peter. 'Oh, look at those fluffy little sheepies!'

Horrid Henry pounced. He was a zombie biting the head off the hapless human.

'AAAAEEEEEE!' squealed Peter.

'Henry!' screamed Mum.

'Stop it!' screamed Dad. 'Or no TV for a week.'

When he was king, thought Horrid Henry, any parent who made their children go on a hike would be dumped barefoot in a scorpion-infested desert.

Plod.
Plod.
Plod.

Horrid Henry dragged his feet. Maybe his horrible mean parents would get fed up waiting for him and turn back, he thought, kicking some mouldy leaves.

Squelch.

Squelch.

Squelch.

Oh no, not *another* muddy meadow.

And then suddenly Horrid Henry had an idea. What was he thinking? All that fresh air must be rotting his brain. The sooner they got to the stupid lake, the sooner they could get home for the *Rapper Zapper Zaps Terminator Gladiator.*

'Come on, everyone, let's run!' shrieked Henry. 'Race you down the hill to the lake!'

'That's the spirit, Henry,' said Dad.

Horrid Henry dashed past Dad.

'OW!' shrieked Dad, tumbling into the stinging nettles.

Horrid Henry
whizzed past Mum.

'Eww!'
shrieked
Mum,
slipping
in a cowpat.

Splat!

Horrid Henry pushed past Peter.

'Waaa!' wailed Peter. 'My wellies are
getting dirty.'

Horrid Henry scampered down the
muddy path.

'Wait Henry!' yelped Mum. 'It's too slipp — aaaiiieeeee!'

Mum slid down the path on her bottom.

'Slow down!' puffed Dad.

'I can't run that fast,' wailed Peter.

But Horrid Henry raced on.

'Shortcut across the field!' he called. 'Come on slowcoaches!' The black and white cow grazing alone in the middle raised its head.

'Henry!' shouted Dad.

Horrid Henry kept running.

'I don't think that's a cow!' shouted Mum.

The cow lowered its head and charged.

'It's a bull!'

yelped Mum and Dad. 'RUN!'

'I said it was dangerous in the country-side!' gasped Henry, as everyone clambered over the stile in the nick of time. 'Look, there's the lake!' he added, pointing.

Henry ran down to the water's edge. Peter followed. The embankment narrowed to a point. Peter slipped past Henry and bagged the best spot, right at the water's edge where the ducks gathered.

'Hey, get away from there,' said Henry.

'I want to feed the ducks,' said Peter.

'*I* want to feed the ducks,' said Henry. 'Now move.'

'I was here first,' said Peter.

'Not any more,' said Henry.

Horrid Henry pushed Peter.

'Out of my way, worm!'

Perfect Peter pushed him back.

'Don't call me worm!'

Henry wobbled.

Peter wobbled.

Splash!

Peter tumbled into the lake.

Crash!

Henry tumbled into the lake.

'My babies!' shrieked Mum, jumping in after them.

'My – glug glug glug!' shrieked Dad, jumping into the muddy water after her.

'My new wellies!' gurgled Perfect Peter.

Bang!

Pow!

Terminator Gladiator slashed at Rapper Zapper.

Zap!

Rapper Zapper slashed back.

'Go Zappy!' yelled Henry, lying bundled up in blankets on the sofa. Once everyone had scrambled out of the lake, Mum and Dad had been keen to get home as fast as possible.

'I think the park next time,' mumbled Dad, sneezing.

'Definitely,' mumbled Mum, coughing.

'Oh, I don't know,' said Horrid Henry happily. 'A little water never hurt anyone.'

2

HORRID HENRY and THE MEGA-MEAN TIME MACHINE

Horrid Henry flicked the switch. The time machine whirred. Dials spun. Buttons pulsed. Latches locked. Horrid Henry Time Traveller was ready for blast off!

Now, where to go, where to go?

Dinosaurs, thought Henry. Yes! Henry loved dinosaurs. He would love to stalk a few Tyrannosaurus Rexes as they rampaged through the primordial jungle.

But what about King Arthur and the Knights of the Round Table? 'Arise, Sir Henry,' King Arthur would say, booting Lancelot out of his chair. 'Sure thing, King,' Sir Henry would reply, twirling his sword. 'Out of my way, worms!'

Or what about the siege of Troy?
Heroic Henry, that's who he'd be, the
fearless fighter dashing about doing daring
deeds.

Tempting, thought Henry. Very tempting.

Wait a sec, what about visiting the
future, where school was banned and
parents had to do whatever their children
told them? Where everyone had their
own spaceship and ate sweets for dinner.
And where King Henry the Horrible
ruled supreme, chopping off the head
of anyone who dared to say no to him.

To the future, thought Henry, setting
the dial.

Bang! Pow!

Henry braced himself for the jolt into
hyperspace – 10, 9, 8, 7, 6 –

'Henry, it's my turn.'

Horrid Henry ignored the alien's whine.

– 5, 4, 3 –

'Henry! If you don't share I'm going to
tell Mum.'

AAAARRRRGGGHHHHHH. The
Time Machine juddered to a halt. Henry
climbed out.

'Go away, Peter,' said Henry. 'You're
spoiling everything.'

'But it's my turn.'

'GO AWAY!'

'Mum said we could *both* play with the

box,' said Peter. 'We could cut out windows, make a little house, paint flowers – '

'NO!' screeched Henry.

'But...' said Peter. He stood in the sitting room, holding his scissors and crayons.

'Don't you touch my box!' hissed Henry.

'I will if I want to,' said Peter. 'And it's not yours.' Henry had no right to boss him around, thought Peter. He'd been waiting such a long time for his turn. Well, he wasn't waiting any longer. He'd start cutting out a window this minute.

Peter got out his scissors.

'Stop! It's a time machine, you toad!' shrieked Henry.

Peter paused.

Peter gasped.

Peter stared at the huge cardboard box. A time machine? *A time machine?* How could it be a time machine?

'It is not,' said Peter.

'Is too,' said Henry.

'But it's made of cardboard,' said Peter. 'And the washing machine came in it.'

Henry sighed.

'Don't you know anything? If it *looked* like a time machine everyone would try to steal it. It's a time machine in *disguise*.'

Peter looked at the time machine. On the one hand he didn't believe Henry for one minute. This was just one of Henry's tricks. Peter was a hundred million billion percent certain Henry was lying.

On the other hand, what if Henry *was* telling the truth for once and there was a real time machine in his sitting room?

'If it *is* a time machine I want to have a go,' said Peter.

'You can't. You're too young,' said Henry.

'Am not.'

'Are too.'

Perfect Peter stuck out his bottom lip.

25

'I don't believe you anyway.'

Horrid Henry was outraged.

'Okay, I'll prove it. I'll go to the future right now. Stand back. Don't move.'

Horrid Henry leapt into the box and closed the lid. The Time Machine began to shudder and shake.

Then everything was still for a very long time.

Perfect Peter didn't know what to do. What if Henry was gone – forever? What if he were stuck in the future?

I could have his room, thought Peter.

I could watch whatever I wanted on telly.
I could –

Suddenly the box tipped over and
Horrid Henry staggered out.

'Wh-wh- where am I?' he stuttered.
Then he collapsed on the floor.

Peter stared at Henry.

Henry stared wildly at Peter.

'I've been to the future!' gasped Henry,
panting. 'It was amazing. Wow. I met
my great-great-great-grandson. He still
lives in this house. And he looks just like
me.'

'So he's ugly,' muttered Peter.

'What – did – you – say?' hissed Henry.

'Nothing,' said Peter quickly. He didn't
know what to think. 'Is this a trick,
Henry?'

'Course it isn't,' said Henry. 'And just
for that I won't let you have a go.'

'I can if I want to,' said Peter.

'You keep away from my time machine,'

said Henry. 'One wrong move and you'll get blasted into the future.'

Perfect Peter walked a few steps towards the time machine. Then he paused.

'What's it like in the future?'

'Boys wear dresses,' said Horrid Henry. 'And lipstick. People talk Ugg language. *You'd* probably like it. Everyone just eats vegetables.'

'Really?'

'And kids have loads of homework.'

Perfect Peter loved homework.

'Ooohh.' This Peter *had* to see. Just in case Henry *was* telling the truth.

'I'm going to the future and you can't stop me,' said Peter.

'Go ahead,' said Henry. Then he snorted. 'You can't go looking like that!'

'Why not?' said Peter.

''Cause everyone will laugh at you.'

Perfect Peter hated people laughing at him.

'Why?'

'Because to them you'll look weird. Are you sure you really want to go to the future?'

'Yes,' said Peter.

'Are you sure you're sure?'

'YES,' said Peter.

'Then I'll get you ready,' said Henry solemnly.

'Thank you, Henry,' said Peter. Maybe he'd been wrong about Henry. Maybe going to the future had turned him into a nice brother.

Horrid Henry dashed out of the sitting room.

Perfect Peter felt a quiver of excitement. The future. What if Henry really was telling the truth?

Horrid Henry returned carrying a large wicker basket. He pulled out an old red dress of Mum's, some lipstick, and a black frothy drink.

'Here, put this on,' said Henry.

Perfect Peter put on the dress. It dragged onto the floor.

'Now, with a bit of lipstick,' said Horrid Henry, applying big blobs of red lipstick all over Peter's face, 'you'll fit right in. Perfect,' he said, standing back to admire his handiwork. 'You look just like a boy from the future.'

'Okay,' said Perfect Peter.

'Now listen carefully,' said Henry.
'When you arrive, you won't be able to
speak the language unless you drink this
bibble babble drink. Take this with you
and drink it when you get there.'

Henry held out the frothy black drink
from his Dungeon Drink Kit. Peter
took it.

'You can now enter the time machine.'
Peter obeyed. His heart was pounding.

'Don't get out until the time machine
has stopped moving completely. Then
count to twenty-five, and open the hatch
very very slowly. You don't want a bit of
you in the twenty-third century, and the

31

rest here in the twenty-first. Good luck.'

Henry swirled the box round and round and round. Peter began to feel dizzy. The drink sloshed on the floor.

Then everything was still.

Peter's head was spinning. He counted to twenty-five, then crept out.

He was in the sitting room of a house that looked just like his. A boy wearing a bathrobe and silver waggly antennae with his face painted in blue stripes stood in front of him.

'Ugg?' said the strange boy.

'Henry?' said Peter.

'Uggg uggg bleuch ble bloop,' said the boy.

'Uggg uggg,' said Peter uncertainly.

'Uggh uggh drink ugggh,' said the boy, pointing to Peter's bibble babble drink.

Peter drank the few drops which were left.

'I'm Zog,' said Zog. 'Who are you?'

'I'm Peter,' said Peter.

'Ahhhhh! Welcome! You must be my great-great-great-uncle Peter. Your very nice brother Henry told me all about you when he visited me from the past.'

'Oh, what did he say?' said Peter.

'That you were an ugly toad.'

'I am not,' said Peter. 'Wait a minute,' he added suspiciously. 'Henry said that boys wore dresses in the future.'

'They do,' said Zog quickly. 'I'm a girl.'

'Oh,' said Peter. He gasped. Henry

would *never* in a million years say he was a girl. Not even if he were being poked with red hot pokers. Could it be. . .

Peter looked around. 'This looks just like my sitting room.'

Zog snorted.

'Of course it does, Uncle Pete. This is now the Peter Museum. You're famous in the future. Everything has been kept exactly as it was.'

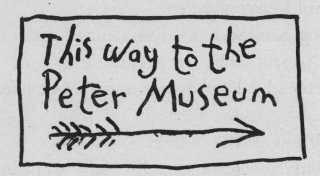

Peter beamed. He was famous in the future. He always knew he'd be famous. A Peter Museum! He couldn't wait to tell Spotless Sam and Tidy Ted.

There was just one more thing . . .

'What about Henry?' he asked. 'Is he famous too?'

'Nah,' said Zog smoothly. 'He's known as What's-His-Name, Peter's older brother.'

Ahh. Peter swelled with pride. Henry was in his lowly place, at last. That proved it. He'd really travelled to the future!

Peter looked out the window. Strange how the future didn't look so different from his own time.

Zog pointed.

'Our spaceships,' he announced.

Peter stared. Spaceships looked just like cars.

'Why aren't they flying?' said Peter.

'Only at night time,' said Zog. 'You can either drive 'em or fly 'em.'

'Wow,' said Peter.

'Don't *you* have spaceships?' said Zog.

'No,' said Peter. 'Cars.'

'I didn't know they had cars in olden

days,' said Zog. 'Do you have blitzkatrons and zappersnappers?'

'No,' said Peter. 'What – '

The front door slammed. Mum walked in. She stared at Peter.

'What on earth. . .'

'Don't be scared,' said Peter. 'I'm Peter. I come from the past. I'm your great-great-great grandfather.'

Mum looked at Peter.

Peter looked at Mum.

'Why are you wearing my dress?' said Mum.

'It's not one of *yours*, silly,' said Peter.

'It belonged to my mum.'

'I see,' said Mum.

'Come on, Uncle Pete,' said Zog quickly, taking Peter firmly by the arm, 'I'll show you our supersonic hammock in the garden.'

'Okay, Zog,' said Peter happily.

Mum beamed.

'It's so lovely to see you playing nicely with your brother, Henry.'

Perfect Peter stood still.

'What did you call him?'

'Henry,' said Mum.

Peter felt a chill.

'So his name's not Zog? And he's not a girl?'

'Not the last time I looked,' said Mum.

'And this house isn't . . . the Peter Museum?'

Mum glared at Henry. 'Henry! Have you been teasing Peter again?'

'Ha ha tricked you!' shrieked Henry.

'Na Na Ne Nah Nah, wait till I tell
everybody!'

'NO!' squealed Peter. 'NOOOOOOO!'
How *could* he have believed his horrible
brother?

'Henry! You horrid boy! Go to your
room! No TV for the rest of the day,' said
Mum.

But Horrid Henry didn't care. The
Mega-Mean Time Machine would go
down in history as his greatest trick ever.

3

PERFECT PETER'S REVENGE

Perfect Peter had had enough. Why oh why did he always fall for Henry's tricks?

Every time it happened he swore Henry would never ever trick him again. And every time he fell for it. How *could* he have believed that there were fairies at the bottom of the garden? Or that there was such a thing as a Fangmangler? But the time machine was the worst. The very very worst. Everyone had teased him. Even Goody-Goody Gordon asked him if he'd seen any spaceships recently.

Well, never again. His mean, horrible brother had tricked him for the very last time.

I'll get my revenge, thought Perfect Peter, pasting the last of his animal stamps into his album. I'll make Henry sorry for being so mean to me.

But what horrid mean nasty thing could he do? Peter had never tried to be revenged on anyone.

He asked Tidy Ted.

'Mess up his room,' said Ted.

But Henry's room was already a mess.

He asked Spotless Sam.

'Put a spaghetti stain on his shirt,' said Sam.

But Henry's shirts were already stained.

Peter picked up a copy of his favourite magazine *Best Boy*. Maybe it would have some handy hints on the perfect revenge. He searched the table of contents:

- IS <u>YOUR</u> BEDROOM AS TIDY AS IT COULD BE?
- TEN TOP TIPS FOR PLEASING YOUR PARENTS
- HOW TO POLISH YOUR TROPHIES

- **WHY MAKING YOUR BED IS GOOD FOR YOU**
- **READERS TELL US ABOUT THEIR FAVOURITE CHORES!**

Reluctantly, Peter closed *Best Boy* magazine. Somehow he didn't think he'd find the answer inside. He was on his own.

I'll tell Mum that Henry eats sweets in his bedroom, thought Peter. Then Henry would get into trouble. Big big trouble.

But Henry got into trouble all the time. That wouldn't be anything special.

I know, thought Peter, I'll hide Mr Kill. Henry would never admit it, but he couldn't sleep without Mr Kill. But so what if Henry couldn't sleep? He'd just come and jump on Peter's head or sneak downstairs and watch scary movies.

I have to think of something really, really horrid, thought Peter. It was hard for Peter to think horrid thoughts, but Peter was determined to try.

He would call Henry a horrid name, like Ugly Toad or Poo Poo face. *That* would show him.

But if I did Henry would hit me, thought Peter.

Wait, he could tell everyone at school that Henry wore nappies. Henry the big nappy. Henry the big smelly nappy. Henry nappy face. Henry poopy pants. Peter smiled happily. That would be a perfect revenge.

Then he stopped smiling. Sadly, no one at school would believe that Henry still wore nappies. Worse, they might think that Peter still did! Eeeek.

I've got it, thought Peter, I'll put a muddy twig in Henry's bed. Peter had read a great story about a younger brother who'd done just that to a mean older one. That would serve Henry right.

But was a muddy twig enough revenge for all of Henry's crimes against him?

No it was not.

I give up, thought Peter, sighing. It was hopeless. He just couldn't think of anything horrid enough.

Peter sat down on his beautifully made bed and opened *Best Boy* magazine.

TELL MUM HOW MUCH YOU LOVE HER!

shrieked the headline.

And then a dreadful thought tiptoed

into his head. It was so dreadful, and so
horrid, that Perfect Peter could not
believe that he had thought it.

'No,' he gasped. 'I couldn't.' That was
too evil.

But . . . but . . . wasn't that exactly what
he wanted? A horrid revenge on a horrid
brother?

'Don't do it!' begged his angel.

'Do it!' urged his devil, thrilled to get
the chance to speak. 'Go on, Peter!

Henry deserves it.'

YES! thought Peter. He would do it.
He would be revenged!

Perfect Peter sat down at the computer.
Tap tap tap.

Dear Margaret,
I love you. Will you marry me?

Peter printed out the note and carefully
scrawled:

HENry

There! thought Peter proudly. That
looks just like Henry's writing. He folded
the note, then sneaked into the garden,
climbed over the wall, and left it on the

table inside Moody Margaret's Secret
Club tent.

'Of course Henry loves me,' said Moody
Margaret, preening. 'He can't help it.
Everyone loves me because I'm so lovable.'

'No you're not,' said Sour Susan. 'You're
moody. And you're mean.'
'Am not!'

'Are too!'

'Am not. You're just jealous 'cause no one would *ever* want to marry you,' snapped Margaret.

'I am not jealous. Anyway, Henry likes *me* the best,' said Susan, waving a folded piece of paper.

'Says who?'

'Says Henry.'

Margaret snatched the paper from Susan's hand and read:

TO THE BEAUTIFUL SUSAN

Oh Susan,
No one is as pretty as you,
You always smell lovely
Just like shampoo.
HENRY

Margaret sniffed. 'Just like dog poo, you mean.'

'I do not,' shrieked Susan.

'Is this your idea of a joke?' snorted Moody Margaret, crumpling the poem.

Sour Susan was outraged.

'No. It was waiting for me on the club-house table. You're just jealous because Henry didn't write *you* a poem.'

'Huh,' said Margaret. Well, she'd show Henry. No one made a fool of her.

Margaret snatched up a pen and scribbled a reply to Henry's note.

'Take this to Henry and report straight back,' she ordered. 'I'll wait here for Linda and Gurinder.'

'Take it yourself,' said Susan sourly. Why oh why was she friends with such a mean, moody jealous grump?

Horrid Henry was inside the Purple Hand Fort plotting death to the Secret Club and scoffing biscuits when an enemy agent peered through the entrance.

'Guard!' shrieked Henry.

But that miserable worm toad was nowhere to be found.

Henry reminded himself to sack Peter immediately.

'Halt! Who goes there?'

'I have an important message,' said the Enemy.

'Make it snappy,' said Henry. 'I'm busy.'

Susan crept beneath the branches.

'Do you really like my shampoo, Henry?' she asked.

Henry stared at Susan. She had a sick smile on her face, as if her stomach hurt.

'Huh?' said Henry.

'You know, my *shampoo*,' said Susan, simpering.

Had Susan finally gone mad?

'*That's* your message?' said Horrid Henry.

'No,' said Susan, scowling. She tossed a scrunched-up piece of paper at Henry and marched off.

Henry opened the note:

I wouldn't marry you if you were the last creature on earth and that includes slimy toads and rattlesnakes. So there.

Margaret

Henry choked on his biscuit. Marry
Margaret?! He'd rather walk around town
carrying a Walkie-Talkie-Burpy-Slurpy-
Teasy-Weasy Doll. He'd rather learn
long division. He'd rather trade all his
computer games for a Princess Pamper
Parlour. He'd rather . . . he'd rather . . .
he'd rather marry Miss Battle-Axe than
marry Margaret!

What on earth had given Margaret the crazy, horrible, revolting idea he wanted to marry *her*?

He always knew Margaret was nuts. Now he had proof. Well well well, thought Horrid Henry gleefully. Wouldn't he tease her! Margaret would never live this down.

Henry leapt over the wall and burst into the Secret Club Tent.

'Margaret, you old pants face, I wouldn't marry you if –'

'Henry loves Margaret! Henry loves Margaret!' chanted Gorgeous Gurinder.

'Henry loves Margaret! Henry loves Margaret!' chanted Lazy Linda, making horrible kissing sounds.

Henry tried to speak. He opened his mouth. Then he closed it.

'No I don't,' gasped Horrid Henry.

'Oh yeah?' said Gurinder.

'Yeah,' said Henry.

'Then why'd you send her a note saying you did?'

'I didn't!' howled Henry.

'And you sent Susan a poem!' said Linda.

'I DID NOT!' howled Henry even louder. What on earth was going on? He took a step backwards.

The Secret Club members advanced on him, shrieking, 'Henry loves Margaret, Henry loves Margaret.'

Time, thought Horrid Henry, to beat a strategic retreat. He dashed back to his fort, the terrible words 'Henry loves Margaret' burning his ears.

'PETER!' bellowed Horrid Henry. 'Come here this minute!'

Perfect Peter crept out of the house to the fort. Henry had found out about the note and the poem. He was dead.

Goodbye, cruel world, thought Peter.

'Did you see anyone going into the Secret Club carrying a note?' demanded Henry, glaring.

Perfect Peter's heart began to beat again.

'No,' said Peter. That wasn't a lie because he hadn't seen himself.

'I want you to stand guard by the wall, and report anyone suspicious to me at once,' said Henry.

'Why?' said Peter innocently.

'None of your business, worm,' snapped Henry. 'Just do as you're told.'

'Yes, Lord High Excellent Majesty of the Purple Hand,' said Perfect Peter. What a lucky escape!

Henry sat on his Purple Hand throne and considered. Who was this foul fiend? Who was this evil genius? Who was spreading these foul rumours? He had to find out, then strike back hard before the snake struck again.

But who'd want to be his enemy? He was such a nice, kind, friendly boy.

True, Rude Ralph wasn't very happy when Henry called him Ralphie Walfie.

Tough Toby wasn't too pleased when Henry debagged him during playtime.

And for some reason, Brainy Brian didn't see the joke when Henry scribbled all over his book report.

Vain Violet said she'd pay Henry back for pulling her pigtails.

And just the other day Fiery Fiona said Henry would be sorry he'd laughed during her speech in assembly.

Even Kind Kasim warned Henry to stop being so horrid or he'd teach him a lesson he wouldn't forget.

But maybe Margaret was behind the whole plot. He had stinkbombed her Secret Club, after all.

Hmmn. The list of suspects was rather long.

It had to be Ralph. Ralph loved playing practical jokes.

Well, it's not funny, Ralph, thought Horrid Henry. Let's see how *you* like it. Perhaps a little poem to Miss Battle-Axe . . .

Horrid Henry grabbed a piece of paper and began to scribble:

Oh Boudicca dear,
Whenever you're near,
I just want to cheer,
Oh big old teacher
Your carrot nose is your best feature
You are so sweet
I would like to kiss your feet
What a treat
Even though they smell of meat
Dear Miss Battle-Axe
Clear out your earwax
So you can hear me say...
No need to frown
But your pants are falling down!

Ha ha ha ha ha,
thought Henry.
He'd sign the
poem 'Ralph', get
to school early and
pin the poem on

the door of the Girls' Toilet. Ralph would
get into big big trouble.

But wait.

What if Ralph *wasn't* responsible?

Could it be Toby after all? Or Margaret?

There was only one thing to do. Henry
copied his poem seven times, signing each
copy with a different name. He would
post them all over school tomorrow. One
of them was sure to be guilty.

Henry sneaked into school, then quickly
pinned up his poems on every notice-
board. That done, he swaggered onto the
playground. Revenge is sweet, thought
Horrid Henry.

There was a crowd gathered outside the
boys' toilets.

'What's going on?' shrieked Horrid
Henry, pushing and shoving his way
through the crowd.

'Henry loves Margaret,' chanted Tough
Toby.

'Henry loves Margaret,' chanted Rude
Ralph.

Uh oh.

Henry glanced at the toilet door. There
was a note taped on it.

**Dear Margaret,
I love you. Will you marry me?**

HENry

Henry's blood froze. He ripped the note off the door.

'Margaret wrote it to herself,' blustered Horrid Henry.

'Didn't!' said Margaret.

'Did!' said Henry.

'Besides, you love *me*!' shrieked Susan.

'No I don't!' shrieked Henry.

'That's 'cause you love me!' said Margaret.

'I hate you!' shouted Henry.

'I hate you more!' said Margaret.

'I hate *you* more,' said Henry.

'You started it,' said Margaret.

'Didn't.'

'Did! You asked me to marry you.'

'NO WAY!' shrieked Henry.

'And you sent me a poem!' said Susan.

'No I didn't!' howled Henry.

'Well, if you didn't then who did?' said Margaret.

Silence.

'Henry,' came a little voice, 'can we play pirates after school today?'

Horrid Henry thought an incredible thought.

Moody Margaret thought an incredible thought.

Sour Susan thought an incredible thought.

Three pairs of eyes stared at Perfect Peter.

'Wha . . . what?' said Peter.

Uh oh.

'HELP!' shrieked Perfect Peter. He turned and ran.

'AAAARRRRGHHHHHH!' shrieked Horrid Henry, chasing after him. 'You're dead meat, worm!'

Miss Battle-Axe marched onto the playground. She was clutching a sheaf of papers in her hand.

'Margaret! Brian! Ralph! Toby! Violet! Kasim! Fiona! What is the meaning of these poems? Straight to the head – now!'

Perfect Peter crashed into her.

Smash!

Miss Battle-Axe toppled backwards into the bin.

'And you too, Peter,' gasped Miss Battle-Axe.

'Waaaaaaa!' wailed Perfect Peter. From now on, he'd definitely be sticking to good deeds. Whoever said revenge was sweet didn't have a horrid brother like Henry.

4

HORRID HENRY DINES AT RESTAURANT LE POSH

'Great news, everyone,' said Mum, beaming. 'Aunt Ruby is taking us all out for dinner to Le Posh, the best French restaurant in town.'

'Oh boy, Restaurant Le Posh,' said Perfect Peter. 'We've never been there.'

Horrid Henry stopped scribbling all over Peter's stamp album. His heart sank. French? Restaurant? Oh no. That meant strange, horrible, yucky food. That meant no burgers, no ketchup, no pizza. That meant —

'NOOOOOOOOOOO! I don't want to

67

go there!' howled Henry. Who knew what revolting poison would arrive on his plate, covered in gloopy sauce with green bits floating about. Uggghh.

'It's Mum's birthday,' said Dad, 'so we're celebrating.'

'I only like Whopper Whoopee,' said Henry. 'Or Fat Frank's. I don't want to go to Le Posh.'

'But Henry,' said Perfect Peter, tidying up his toys, 'it's a chance to try new food.'

Mum beamed. 'Quite right, Peter. It's always nice to try new things.'

'No it isn't,' snarled Horrid Henry. 'I hate trying new food when there's nothing wrong with the old.'

'I love it,' said Dad. 'I eat everything except tomatoes.'

'And I eat everything except squid,' said Mum.

'And I love all vegetables except beetroot,' said Perfect Peter. 'Especially spinach and sprouts.'

'Well I don't,' shrieked Horrid Henry. 'Do they have pasta?'

'Whatever they have will be delicious,' said Mum firmly.

'Do they have burgers? If they don't I'm not going,' wailed Horrid Henry.

Mum looked at Dad.

Dad looked at Mum.

Last time they'd taken Henry to a fancy restaurant he'd had a tantrum under the table. The time before he'd run screaming round the room snatching all the salt and pepper shakers and then thrown up on the people at the next table. The time

before that — Mum and Dad preferred not to think about that.

'Shall we get a babysitter?' murmured Dad.

'Leave him home on my birthday?' murmured Mum. She allowed herself to be tempted for a moment. Then she sighed.

'Henry, you are coming and you will be on your best behaviour,' said Mum. 'Your cousin Steve will be there. You wouldn't want Steve to see you make a fuss, would you?'

The hairs on the back of Henry's neck stood up. Steve! Stuck-Up Steve! Horrid Henry's arch-enemy and world's worst cousin. If there was a slimier boy than Steve slithering around then Horrid Henry would eat worms.

Last time they'd met Henry had tricked Steve into thinking there was a monster under his bed. Steve had sworn revenge. There was nothing Steve wouldn't do to get back at Henry.

Boy, did Horrid Henry hate Stuck-Up Steve.

Boy, did Stuck-Up Steve hate Horrid Henry.

'I'm not coming and that's final!' screamed Horrid Henry.

'Henry,' said Dad. 'I'll make a deal with you.'

'What deal?' said Henry. It was always wise to be suspicious when parents offered deals.

'I want you to be pleasant and talk to everyone. And you will eat everything on your plate like everyone else without making a fuss. If you do, I'll give you £2.'

£2! Two whole pounds! Horrid Henry gasped. Two whole pounds just for talking

and shoving a few
mouthfuls of
disgusting
food in his
mouth.

Normally he had to do that for free.

'How about £3?' said Henry.

'Henry . . .' said Mum.

'OK, deal,' said Horrid Henry. But I
won't eat a thing and they can't make me,
he thought. He'd find a way. Dad said he
had to eat everything on his plate. Well,
maybe some food wouldn't *stay* on his
plate. . . Horrid Henry smiled.

Perfect Peter stopped putting away his
bricks. He frowned. Shouldn't *he* get two
pounds like Henry?

'What's *my* reward for being good?' said
Perfect Peter.

'Goodness is its own reward,' said Dad.

★

The restaurant was hushed. The tables were covered in snowy-white tablecloths, with yellow silk chairs. Huge gold chandeliers dangled from the ceiling. Crystal glasses twinkled. The rectangular china plates sparkled. Horrid Henry was impressed.

'Wow,' said Henry. It was like walking into a palace.

'Haven't you ever been here before?' sneered Stuck-Up Steve.

'No,' said Henry.

'*We* eat here all the time,' said Steve. 'I guess you're too poor.'

'It's 'cause *we'd* rather eat at Whopper Whoopee,' lied Henry.

'Hush, Steve,' said Rich Aunt Ruby. 'I'm sure Whopper Whoopee is a lovely restaurant.'

Steve snorted.

Henry kicked him under the table.

'OWWWW!' yelped Steve. 'Henry kicked me!'

'No I didn't,' said Henry. 'It was an accident.'

'Henry,' said Mum through gritted teeth. 'Remember what we said about best behaviour? We're in a fancy restaurant.'

Horrid Henry scowled. He looked cautiously around. It was just as he'd feared. Everyone was busy eating weird

bits of this and that, covered in gloopy
sauces. Henry checked under the tables to
see if anyone was being sick yet.

There was no one lying poisoned under
the tables. I guess it's just a matter of time,
thought Henry grimly. You won't catch
me eating anything here.

Mum, Dad, Peter and Rich Aunt Ruby
blabbed away at their end of the table.
Horrid Henry sat sullenly next to Stuck-
Up Steve.

'I've got a new bike,' Steve bragged. 'Do you still have that old rust bucket you had last Christmas?'

'Hush, Steve,' said Rich Aunt Ruby.

Horrid Henry's foot got ready to kick Steve.

'Boudicca Battle-Axe! How many times have I told you — don't chew with your mouth open,' boomed a terrible voice.

Horrid Henry looked up. His jaw dropped.

There was his terrifying teacher, Miss Battle-Axe, sitting at a small table in the corner with her back to him. She was with someone even taller, skinnier, and

more ferocious than she was.

'And take your elbows off the table!'

'Yes, Mum,' said Miss Battle-Axe meekly.

Henry could not believe his ears. Did teachers have mothers? Did teachers ever leave the school? Impossible.

'Boudicca! Stop slouching!'

'Yes, Mum,' said Miss Battle-Axe, straightening up a fraction.

'So, what's everyone having?' beamed Aunt Ruby. Horrid Henry tore his eyes away from Miss Battle-Axe and stared at

the menu. It was entirely written in French.

'I recommend the mussels,' said Aunt Ruby.

'Mussels! Ick!' shrieked
Henry.

'Or the blah
blah blah blah
blah.' Aunt Ruby
pronounced a few
mysterious French words.

'Maybe,' said Mum. She looked a little
uncertain.

'Maybe,' said Dad. He looked a little
uncertain.

'You order for me, Aunt Ruby,' said
Perfect Peter. 'I eat everything.'

Horrid Henry had no idea what food
Aunt Ruby had suggested, but he knew
he hated every single thing on the menu.

'I want a burger,' said Henry.

'No burgers here,' said Mum firmly.
'This is Restaurant Le Posh.'

'I said I want a burger!' shouted Henry.
Several diners looked up.

'Don't be horrid Henry!' hissed Mum.

'I CAN'T UNDERSTAND THIS MENU!' screamed Henry.

'Calm down this minute Henry,' hissed Dad. 'Or no £2.'

Mum translated: 'A tasty . . . uh . . . something on a bed of roast something with a something sauce.'

'Sounds delicious,' said Dad.

'Wait, there's more,' said Mum. 'A big piece of something enrobed with some-thing cooked in something with carrots.'

'Right, I'm having that,' said Dad. 'I love carrots.'

Mum carried on translating. Henry opened his mouth to scream –

'Why don't you order *tripe*?' said Steve.

'What's that?' asked Henry suspiciously.

'You don't want to know,' said Steve.

'Try me,' said Henry.

'Intestines,' said Steve. 'You know, the wriggly bits in your stomach.'

Horrid Henry snorted. Sometimes he felt sorry for Steve. Did Steve really think he'd fool him with *that* old trick? *Tripe* was probably a fancy French word for spaghetti. Or trifle.

'Or you could order *escargots*,' said Steve. 'I dare you.'

'What's *escargots*?' said Henry.

Stuck-Up Steve stuck his nose in the air.

'Oh, sorry, I forgot you don't learn French at your school. *I've* been learning it for years.'

'Whoopee for you,' said Horrid Henry.

'*Escargots* are snails, stupid,' said Stuck-Up Steve.

Steve must think he was a real idiot, thought Horrid Henry indignantly. *Snails*. Ha ha ha. In a restaurant? As if.

'Oh yeah, right, you big fat liar,' said Henry.

Steve shrugged.

'Too chicken, huh?' he sneered. 'Cluck cluck cluck.'

Horrid Henry was outraged. No one called him chicken and lived.

'Course not,' said Horrid Henry. 'I'd love to eat snails.' Naturally it would turn out to be fish or something in a smelly, disgusting sauce, but so what? *Escargots* could hardly be more revolting than all the other yucky things on the menu. Steve would have to try harder than that to fool him. He would order so-called 'snails' just to show Steve up for the liar he was. Then wouldn't he make fun of stupid old Steve!

'And vat are ve having tonight?' asked the French waiter.

Aunt Ruby ordered.

'An excellent choice, madame,' said the waiter.

Dad ordered. The waiter kissed his fingers.

'*Magnifique*, monsieur, our speciality.'

Mum ordered.

'Bravo, madame. And what about you, young man?' the waiter asked Henry.

'I'm having *escargots*,' said Henry.

'Hmmn,' said the waiter. 'Monsieur is a gourmet?'

Horrid Henry wasn't sure he liked the sound of that. Stuck-Up Steve snickered. What was going on? thought Horrid Henry.

'Boudicca! Eat your vegetables!'

'Yes, Mum.'

'Boudicca! Stop slurping.'

'Yes, Mum,' snapped Miss Battle-Axe.

'Boudicca! Don't pick your nose!'

'I wasn't!' said Miss Battle-Axe.

'Don't you contradict me,' said Mrs Battle-Axe.

The waiter reappeared, carrying six plates covered in silver domes.

'Voilà!' he said, whisking off the lids with a flourish. 'Bon appétit!'

Everyone peered at their elegant plates.

'Ah,' said Mum, looking at her squid.

'Ah,' said Dad, looking at his stuffed tomatoes.

'Ah,' said Peter, looking at his beetroot mousse.

Horrid Henry stared at his food. It
looked like — it couldn't be — oh my
God, it was . . . SNAILS! It really was
snails! Squishy squashy squidgy slimy
slithery slippery snails. Still in their shells.
Drenched in butter, but unmistakably
snails. Steve had tricked him.

Horrid Henry's hand reached out to
hurl the snails at Steve.

Stuck-Up Steve giggled.

Horrid Henry stopped and gritted his teeth. No way was he giving Steve the satisfaction of seeing him get into big trouble. He'd ordered snails and he'd eat snails. And when he threw up, he'd make sure it was all over Steve.

Horrid Henry grabbed his fork and plunged. Then he closed his eyes and popped the snail in his mouth.

Horrid Henry chewed.

Horrid Henry chewed some more.

'Hmmn,' said Horrid Henry.

He popped another snail in his mouth. And another.

'Yummy,' said Henry. 'This is brilliant.'
Why hadn't anyone told him that Le Posh
served such thrillingly revolting food?
Wait till he told Rude Ralph!

Stuck-Up Steve looked unhappy.

'How's your maggot sauce, Steve?' said
Henry cheerfully.

'It's not maggot sauce,' said Steve.

'Maggot maggot maggot,' whispered
Henry. 'Watch them wriggle about.'

Steve put down his fork. So did Mum,
Dad, and Peter.

'Go on everyone, eat up,' said Henry,
chomping.

'I'm not that hungry,' said Mum.

'You said we had to eat everything on
our plate,' said Henry.

'No I didn't,' said Dad weakly.

'You did too!' said Henry. 'So eat!'

'I don't like beetroot,' moaned Perfect
Peter.

'Hush, Peter,' snapped Mum.

'Peter, I never thought *you* were a fussy eater,' said Aunt Ruby.

'I'm not!' wailed Perfect Peter.

'Boudicca!' blasted Mrs Battle-Axe's shrill voice. 'Pay attention when I'm speaking to you!'

'Yes, Mum,' said Miss Battle-Axe.

'Why can't you be as good as that boy?' said Mrs Battle-Axe, pointing to Horrid Henry. 'Look at him sitting there, eating so beautifully.'

Miss Battle-Axe turned round and saw Henry. Her face went bright red, then

purple, then white. She gave him a sickly smile.

Horrid Henry gave her a little polite wave. Oh boy.

For the first time in his life was he ever looking forward to school.

HORRID HENRY
AND THE
FOOTBALL FIEND

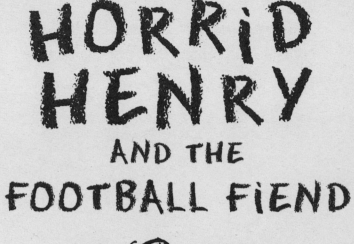

To Elaine and Mark Eisenthal,
and to Alexander, Josh and Katherine

CONTENTS

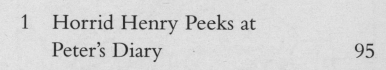

1

HORRID HENRY PEEKS AT PETER'S DIARY

'What are you doing?' demanded Horrid Henry, bursting into Peter's bedroom.

'Nothing,' said Perfect Peter quickly, slamming his notebook shut.

'Yes you are,' said Henry.

'Get out of my room,' said Peter. 'You're not allowed to come in unless I say so.'

Horrid Henry leaned over Peter's shoulder.

'What are you writing?'

'None of your business,' said Peter. He

covered the closed notebook tightly
with his arm.

'It is *too* my business if you're writing
about *me*.'

'It's *my* diary. I can write what I want
to,' said Peter. 'Miss Lovely said we
should keep a diary for a week and
write in it every day.'

'Bo-ring,' said Henry, yawning.

'No it isn't,' said Peter. 'Anyway, you'll
find out next week what I'm writing:
I've been chosen to read my diary out
loud for our class assembly.'

Horrid Henry's heart turned to ice.

Peter read his diary out loud? So the
whole school could hear Peter's lies
about him? No way!

'Gimme that!' screamed Horid Henry,
lunging for the diary.

'No!' screamed Peter, holding on tight.
'MUUUM! Help! Henry's in my room!

And he didn't knock! And he won't leave!'

'Shut up, tattle-tale,' hissed Henry, forcing Peter's fingers off the diary.

'MUUUUMMMMMM!' shrieked Peter.

Mum stomped up the stairs.

Henry opened the diary. But before he could read a single word Mum burst in.

'He snatched my diary! And he told me to shut up!' wailed Peter.

'Henry! Stop annoying your brother,' said Mum.

'I wasn't,' said Henry.

'Yes he was,' snivelled Peter.

'And now you've made him cry,' said Mum. 'Say sorry.'

'I was just asking about his homework,' protested Henry innocently.

'He was trying to read my diary,' said Peter.

'Henry!' said Mum. 'Don't be horrid. A diary is private. Now leave your brother alone.'

It was so unfair. Why did Mum always believe Peter?

Humph. Horrid Henry stalked out of Peter's bedroom. Well, no way was Henry waiting until class assembly to find out what Peter had written.

Sneak. Sneak. Sneak.

Horrid Henry checked to the right. Horrid Henry checked to the left. Mum was downstairs working on the computer.

Dad was in the garden. Peter was playing at Goody-Goody Gordon's house.

At last, the coast was clear. He'd been trying to get hold of Peter's diary for days. There was no time to lose.

Tomorrow was Peter's class assembly. Would he mention Sunday's food fight, when Henry had been forced to throw soggy pasta at Peter? Or when Henry had to push Peter off the comfy black chair and pinch him? Or yesterday when Henry banished him from the

Purple Hand Club and Peter had run scream- ing to Mum?

A lying, slimy worm like Peter would be sure to make it look like Henry was the villain when in fact Peter was always to blame.

Even worse, what horrid lies had Peter been making up about him? People would read Peter's ravings and think they were true. When Henry was famous, books would be written about him, and someone would find Peter's diary and believe it! When things were written down they had a horrible way of seeming to be true even when they were big fat lies.

Henry sneaked into Peter's bedroom

and shut the door. Now, where was that diary? Henry glanced at Peter's tidy desk. Peter kept it on the second shelf, next to his crayons and trophies.

The diary was gone.

Rats. Peter must have hidden it.

That little worm, thought Horrid Henry. Why on earth would he hide his diary? And *where* on earth would that smelly toad hide it? Behind his 'Good as Gold' certificates? In the laundry basket? Underneath his stamp collection?

He checked Peter's sock drawer. No diary.

He checked Peter's underwear drawer.
No diary.

He peeked under Peter's pillow, and
under Peter's bed.

Still no diary.

OK, where would *I* hide a diary,
thought Horrid Henry desperately. Easy.
I'd put it in a chest and bury it in the
garden, with a pirate curse on it.

Somehow he doubted
Perfect Peter would
be so clever.

OK, thought
Henry, if I were an
ugly toad like him, where would I hide
it?

The bookcase. Of course. What better
place to hide a book?

Henry strolled over to Peter's
bookcase, with all the books arranged
neatly in alphabetical order. Aha! What

was that sticking out between *The Happy Nappy* and *The Hoppy Hippo*?

Gotcha, thought Horrid Henry, yanking the diary off the shelf. At last he would know Peter's secrets. He'd make him cross out all his lies if it was the last thing he did.

Horrid Henry sat down and began to read:

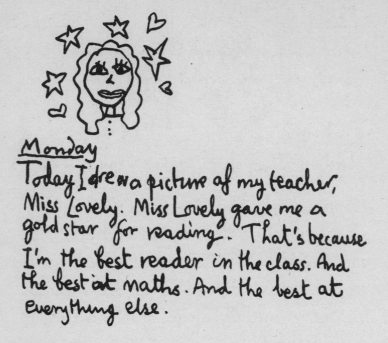

<u>Monday</u>
Today I drew a picture of my teacher,
Miss Lovely. Miss Lovely gave me a
gold star for reading. That's because
I'm the best reader in the class. And
the best at maths. And the best at
everything else.

<u>Tuesday</u>
Today I said please and thank you
236 times

<u>Wednesday</u>
Today I ate all my vegetables

Thursday
Today I sharpened my pencils.
I ate all my sprouts and had
seconds.

Friday
Today I wrote a poem to my mummy
    I love my mummy,
    I came out of her tummy,
    Her food is yummy,
    She is so scrummy,
    I love my mummy.

Slowly Horrid Henry closed Peter's diary. He knew Peter's diary would be bad. But never in his worst nightmares had he imagined anything this bad.

Perfect Peter hadn't mentioned him once. Not once.

You'd think I didn't even live in this house, thought Henry. He was outraged.

105

How dare Peter *not* write about him?
And then all the stupid things Peter *had*
written.

Henry's name would be mud when
people heard Peter's diary in assembly
and found out what a sad brother he
had. Everyone would tease him. Horrid
Henry would never live down the
shame.

Peter needed Henry's help, and he
needed it fast. Horrid Henry grabbed a
pencil and got to work.

<u>Monday</u>
Today I drew a picture of my teacher,
Miss Lovely. I drew her with piggy
ears and a grate big giant belly
Then I turned it into a
dartbord. Miss Lovely gave me
a gold star for reading. Miss
Lovely is my worst teecher
ever. She should reely be
called Miss Lumpy.
Miss Dumpy Lumpy is wot Gordon
and I call her behind her back.
Tee hee, she'll never know!

I'm the best reader in the class. And

the best at maths. And the best at everything else. Too bad I have smelly pants and nitty hair

That's more like it, thought Horrid Henry.

Tuesday
Today I said please and thank you 236 times

~~To~~ Not! I called Mum a big blobby pants face. I called Dad a stinky fish. Then I played Pirats with the worlds greatest brother, Henry. I Wish I were as clever as Henry. But I know thats imposibel.

Wednesday
Today I ate all my vegetables

then I sneaked loads of sweets from the sweet Jar and lied to dad about it. I am a very good liar. No one should ever beleeve a word I say. Henry gets the blame but reely every thing is always my fault.

Thursday
Today I sharpened my pencils.

All the better to write rude notes!

I ate all my sprouts and had seconds. then threw up all over Mum. Eeugh, what a smell. I reelly am a smelly toad. I am so lucky to have a grate brother like Henry. He is always so nice to me Hip Hip Hurray for Henry

Friday
Today I wrote a poem to my Dummy

I Love my Dummy,
It's my best chummy
It tastes so yummy,
It is so scrummy,
I love my Dummy.

Much better, thought Horrid Henry. Now that's what I call a diary. Everyone would have died of boredom otherwise.

Henry carefully replaced Peter's diary in the bookcase. I hope Peter appreciates what I've done for him, thought Horrid Henry.

The entire school gathered in the hall for assembly. Peter's class sat proudly on benches at the front. Henry's class sat cross-legged on the floor. The parents sat on chairs down both sides.

Mum and Dad waved at Peter. He waved shyly back.

Miss Lovely stood up.

'Hello Mums and Dads, boys and girls, welcome to our class assembly. This term our class has been keeping diaries. We're going to read some of them to you now. First to read will be Peter. Everyone pay attention, and see if you too can be as good as I know Peter has been. I'd like everyone here to copy one of Peter's good deeds. I know I can't wait to hear how he has spent this last week.'

Peter stood up, and opened his diary. In a big loud voice, he read:

'MONDAY

'Today I drew a picture of my teacher, Miss Lovely.'

Peter glanced up at Miss Lovely. She beamed at him.

'I drew her with piggy ears and a
great big giant belly. Then I
turned it into a
dartboard.'

What??! It was always difficult to read
out loud and understand what he had
read, but something didn't sound right.
He didn't remember writing about a pig
with a big belly. Nervously Peter looked
up at Mum and Dad. Was he imagining
it, or did their smiles seem more like

112

frowns? Peter shook his head, and carried on.

'Miss Lovely gave me a gold star for reading,'

Phew, that was better! He must have misheard himself before.

'Miss Lovely is my worst teacher ever. She should really be called Miss Lumpy. Miss Dumpy Lumpy—'

'Thank you, that's quite enough,' interrupted Miss Lovely sternly, as the school erupted in shrieks of laughter. Her face was pink. 'Peter, see me after assembly. Ted will now tell us all about skeletons.'

'But—but—' gasped Perfect Peter. 'I—I didn't, I never—'

'Sit down and be quiet,' said the head, Mrs Oddbod. 'I'll see you *and* your parents later.'

'WAAAAAAAAAA!' wailed Peter.

Mum and Dad stared at their feet. Why had they ever had children? Where was a trapdoor when you needed one?

'Waaaaaaaa,' whimpered Mum and Dad.

Naturally, Henry got into trouble. Big big trouble. It was so unfair. Why didn't anyone believe him when he said he'd improved Peter's diary for his own good? Honestly, he would never *ever* do Peter a favour again.

HORRID HENRY AND THE FOOTBALL FIEND

'...AND with 15 seconds to go it's Hot-Foot Henry racing across the pitch! Rooney tries a slide tackle but Henry's too quick! Just look at that step-over! Oh no, he can't score from that distance, it's crazy, it's impossible, oh my goodness, he cornered the ball, it's IN!!!! It's IN! Another *spectacular* goal! Another spectacular win! And it's all thanks to Hot-Foot Henry, the greatest footballer who's ever lived!'

'Goal! Goal! Goal!' roared the crowd.
Hot-Foot Henry had won the match!
His teammates carried him through the
fans, cheering and chanting, 'Hen-ry!
Hen-ry! Hen-ry!'

'HENRY!'

Horrid Henry looked up to see Miss
Battle-Axe leaning over his table and
glaring at him with her red eyes.

'What did I just say?'

'Henry,' said Horrid Henry.

Miss Battle-Axe scowled.

'I'm watching you, Henry,' she
snapped. 'Now class, please pay
attention, we need to discuss—'

'Waaaaa!' wailed Weepy
William.

'Susan, stop
pulling my
hair!' squealed
Vain Violet.

'Miss!' shouted Inky Ian, 'Ralph's snatched my pen!'

'Didn't!' shouted Rude Ralph.

'Did!' shouted Inky Ian.

'Class! Be quiet!' bellowed Miss Battle-Axe.

'Waaaaa!' wailed Weepy William.

'Owwww!' squealed Vain Violet.

'Give it back!' shouted Inky Ian.

'Fine,' said Miss Battle-Axe, 'we won't talk about football.'

William stopped wailing.

Violet stopped squealing.

Ian stopped shouting.

Henry stopped daydreaming.

Everyone in the class stared at Miss Battle-Axe. Miss Battle-Axe wanted to talk about . . . football? Was this an alien Miss Battle-Axe?

'As you all know, our local team, Ashton Athletic, has reached the sixth round of the FA Cup,' said Miss Battle-Axe.

'YEY!' shrieked the class.

'And I'm sure you all know what happened last night . . .'

Last night! Henry could still hear the announcer's glorious words as he and Peter had gathered round the radio as the draw for round six was announced.

'Number 16, Ashton Athletic, will be playing . . .' there was a long pause as the announcer drew another ball from the hat . . . 'number 7, Manchester United.'

'Go Ashton!' shrieked Horrid Henry.

'As I was saying, before I was so rudely interrupted—' Miss Battle-Axe glared at Horrid Henry, 'Ashton are playing Manchester United in a few weeks. Every local primary school has been given a pair of tickets. And thanks to my good luck in the teacher's draw, the lucky winner will come from our class.'

'Me!' screamed Horrid Henry.

'Me!' screamed Moody Margaret.

'Me!' screamed Tough Toby, Aerobic

121

Al, Fiery Fiona and Brainy Brian.

'No one who shouts out will be getting anything,' said Miss Battle-Axe. 'Our class will be playing a football match at lunchtime. The player of the match will win the tickets. I'm the referee and my decision will be final.'

Horrid Henry was so stunned that for a moment he could scarcely breathe. FA Cup tickets! FA Cup tickets to see his local team Ashton play against Man U! Those tickets were like gold dust. Henry had begged and pleaded with Mum and Dad to get tickets, but naturally they were all sold out by the time Henry's mean, horrible, lazy parents managed to heave their stupid bones to the phone. And now here was another chance to go to the match of the century!

Ashton Athletic had never got so far in the Cup. Sure, they'd knocked out the Tooting Tigers (chant: Toot Toot! Grrr!) the Pynchley Pythons and the Cheam Champions but—Manchester United! Henry had to go to the game. He just had to. And all he had to do was be man of the match.

There was just one problem. Unfortunately, the best footballer in the class wasn't Horrid Henry. Or Aerobic Al. Or Beefy Bert.

The best footballer in the class was Moody Margaret. The second best player in the class was Moody Margaret. The third best player in the class was

Moody Margaret. It was so unfair! Why should Margaret of all people be so fantastic at football?

Horrid Henry was brilliant at shirt pulling. Horrid Henry was superb at

screaming 'Offside!' (whatever that meant). No one could howl 'Come on, ref!' louder. And at toe-treading, elbowing, barging, pushing, shoving and tripping, Horrid Henry had no equal. The only thing Horrid Henry wasn't good at was playing football.

But never mind. Today would be different. Today he would dig deep inside and find the power to be Hot-Foot Henry—for real. Today no one would stop him. FA Cup match here I come, thought Horrid Henry gleefully.

Lunchtime!

Horrid Henry's class dashed to the back playground, where the pitch was set up. Two jumpers either end marked the goals. A few parents gathered on the sidelines.

Miss Battle-Axe split the class into

two teams: Aerobic Al was captain of Henry's team, Moody Margaret was captain of the other.

There she stood in midfield, having nabbed a striker position, smirking confidently. Horrid Henry glared at her from the depths of the outfield.

'Na na ne nah nah, I'm sure to be man of the match,' trilled Moody Margaret, sticking out her tongue at him. 'And you-ooo won't.'

'Shut up, Margaret,' said Henry. When he was king, anyone named Margaret would be boiled in oil and fed to the crows.

'Will you take me to the match, Margaret?' said Susan. 'After all, *I'm* your best friend.'

Moody Margaret scowled. 'Since when?'

'Since always!' wailed Susan.

'Huh!' said Margaret. 'We'll just have to see how nice you are to me, won't we?'

'Take me,' begged Brainy Brian. 'Remember how I helped you with those fractions?'

'And called me stupid,' said Margaret.

'Didn't,' said Brian.

'Did,' said Margaret.

Horrid Henry eyed his classmates.

Everyone looking straight ahead, everyone determined to be man of the match. Well, wouldn't they be in for a shock when Horrid Henry waltzed off with those tickets!

'Go Margaret!' screeched Moody Margaret's mum.

'Go Al!' screeched Aerobic Al's dad.

'Everyone ready?' said Miss Battle-Axe. 'Bert! Which team are you on?'

'I dunno,' said Beefy Bert.

Miss Battle-Axe blew her whistle.

Kick-off!

Kick.

Chase.

Kick.

Dribble.

Dribble.

Pass.

Kick.

Save!

Goal Kick

Henry stood disconsolately on the left wing, running back and forth as the play passed him by. How could he ever be man of the match stuck out here? Well, no way was he staying in this stupid spot a moment longer.

Horrid Henry abandoned his position and chased after the ball. All the other defenders followed him.

Moody Margaret had the ball. Horrid Henry ran up behind her. He glanced at Miss Battle-Axe. She was busy chatting to Mrs Oddbod. Horrid Henry went for a two foot slide tackle and tripped her.

'Foul!' screeched Margaret. 'He hacked my leg!'

'Liar!' screeched Henry. 'I just went for the ball!'

'Cheater!' screamed Moody Margaret's mum.

'Play on,' ordered Miss Battle-Axe.

Yes! thought Horrid Henry triumphantly. After all, what did blind old Miss Battle-Axe know about the rules of football? Nothing. This was his golden chance to score.

Now Jazzy Jim had the ball.

Horrid Henry trod on his toes, elbowed him, and grabbed the ball.

'Hey, we're on the same team!' yelped Jim.

Horrid Henry kept dribbling.

'Pass! Pass!' screamed Al. 'Man on!'

Henry ignored him. Pass the ball? Was Al mad? For once Henry had the ball and he was keeping it.

Then suddenly Moody Margaret
appeared from behind, barged him,
dribbled the ball past Henry's team and
kicked it straight past Weepy William
into goal. Moody Margaret's team
cheered.

Weepy William burst into tears.

'Waaaaaa,' wailed Weepy William.

'Idiot!' screamed Aerobic Al's dad.

'She cheated!' shrieked Henry. 'She
fouled me!'

'Didn't,' said Margaret.

'How dare you call my daughter a
cheater?' screamed
Margaret's mum.

Miss Battle-
Axe blew her
whistle.

'Goal to
Margaret's team. The
score is one-nil.'

Horrid Henry gritted his teeth. He would score a goal if he had to trample on every player to do so.

Unfortunately, everyone else seemed to have the same idea.

'Ralph pushed me!' shrieked Aerobic Al.

'Didn't!' lied Rude Ralph. 'It was just a barge.'

'He used his hands, I saw him!' howled Al's father. 'Send him off.'

'I'll send *you* off if you don't behave,' snapped Miss Battle-Axe, looking up and blowing her whistle.

'It was kept in!' protested Henry.

'No way!' shouted Margaret. 'It went past the line!'

'That was ball to hand!' yelled Kind Kasim.

'No way!' screamed Aerobic Al. 'I just went for the ball.'

'Liar!'

'Liar!'

'Free kick to Margaret's team,' said Miss Battle-Axe.

'Ouch!' screamed Soraya, as Brian stepped on her toes, grabbed the ball, and headed it into goal past Kasim.

'Hurray!' cheered Al's team.

'Foul!' screamed Margaret's team.

'Score is one all,' said Miss Battle-Axe. 'Five more minutes to go.'

AAARRRGGHH! thought Horrid Henry. I've got to score a goal to have a chance to be man of the match. I've just got to. But how, how?

Henry glanced at Miss Battle-Axe. She appeared to be rummaging in her handbag. Henry saw his chance. He stuck out his foot as Margaret hurtled past.

Crash!

Margaret tumbled.

Henry seized the ball.

'Henry hacked my leg!' shrieked Margaret.

'Did not!' shrieked Henry. 'I just went for the ball.'

'REF!' screamed Margaret.

'He cheated!' screamed Margaret's mum. 'Are you blind, ref?'

Miss Battle-Axe glared.

'My eyesight is perfect, thank you,' she snapped.

Tee hee, chortled Horrid Henry.

Henry trod on Brian's toes, elbowed him, then grabbed the ball. Then Dave elbowed Henry, Ralph trod on Dave's toes, and Susan seized the ball and kicked it high overhead.

Henry looked up. The ball was high, high up. He'd never reach it, not unless, unless— Henry glanced at Miss Battle-Axe. She was watching a traffic warden patrolling outside the school gate. Henry leapt into the air and whacked the ball with his hand.

Thwack!

The ball hurled across the goal.

'Goal!' screamed Henry.

'He used his hands!' protested Margaret.

'No way!' shouted Henry. 'It was the hand of God!'

'Hen-ry! Hen-ry! Hen-ry!' cheered his team.

'Unfair!' howled Margaret's team.

Miss Battle-Axe blew her whistle.

'Time!' she bellowed. 'Al's team wins 2-1.'

'Yes!' shrieked Horrid Henry, punching the air. He'd scored the winning goal! He'd be man of the match! Ashton Athletic versus Man U here I come!

Horrid Henry's class limped through the door and sat down. Horrid Henry sat at the front, beaming. Miss Battle-Axe had to award him the tickets after his brilliant performance and spectacular, game-winning goal. The question was, who *deserved* to be his guest?

No one.

I know, thought Horrid Henry, I'll sell my other ticket. Bet I get a million pounds for it. No, a billion pounds. Then I'll buy my own team, and play striker any time I want to. Horrid Henry smiled happily.

Miss Battle-Axe glared at her class.

'That was absolutely disgraceful,' she said. 'Cheating! Moving the goals! Shirt tugging!' she glared at Graham. 'Barging!

She glowered at Ralph. 'Pushing and shoving! Bad sportsmanship!' Her eyes swept over the class.

Horrid Henry sank lower in his seat. Oops.

'And don't get me started about offside,' she snapped.

Horrid Henry sank even lower.

'There was only one person who deserves to be player of the match,' she continued. 'One person who observed the rules of the beautiful game. One person who has nothing to be ashamed of today.'

Horrid Henry's heart leapt. *He* certainly had nothing to be ashamed of.

'. . . One person who can truly be proud of their performance . . .'

Horrid Henry beamed with pride.

'And that person is—'

'Me! screamed Moody Margaret.

'Me!' screamed Aerobic Al.

'Me! screamed Horrid Henry.

'—the referee,' said Miss Battle-Axe.

What?

Miss Battle-Axe . . . man of the match?

Miss Battle-Axe . . . a football fiend?

'IT'S NOT FAIR!' screamed the class.

'IT'S NOT FAIR!' screamed Horrid Henry.

3

HORRID HENRY GOES SHOPPING

Horrid Henry stood in his bedroom up to his knees in clothes. The long sleeve stripy T-shirt came to his elbow. His trousers stopped halfway down his legs. Henry sucked in his tummy as hard as he could. Still the zip wouldn't zip.

'Nothing fits!' he screamed, yanking off the shirt and hurling it across the room. 'And my shoes hurt.'

'All right Henry, calm down,' said Mum. 'You've grown. We'll go out this afternoon and get you some new clothes and shoes.'

'NOOOOOOO!' shrieked Henry.
'NOOOOOOOOOOOOO!'

Horrid Henry hated shopping.

Correction: Horrid Henry loved
shopping. He loved shopping for
gigantic TVs, computer games, comics,
toys, and sweets. Yet for some reason
Horrid Henry's parents never wanted to
go shopping for good stuff. Oh no. They
shopped for hoover bags. Toothpaste.
Spinach. Socks. Why oh why did he
have such horrible parents? When he
was grown-up he'd never set foot in a

supermarket. He'd only shop for TVs, computer games, and chocolate.

But shopping for clothes was even worse than heaving his heavy bones round the Happy Shopper Supermarket. Nothing was more boring than being dragged round miles and miles and miles of shops, filled with disgusting clothes only a mutant would ever want to wear, and then standing in a little room while Mum made you try on icky scratchy things you wouldn't be seen dead in if they were the last trousers on earth. It was horrible enough getting dressed once a day without doing it fifty times. Just thinking about trying on shirt after shirt after shirt made Horrid Henry want to scream.

'I'm not going shopping!' he howled, kicking the pile of clothes as viciously as he could. 'And you can't make me.'

'What's all this yelling?' demanded Dad.

'Henry needs new trousers,' said Mum grimly.

Dad went pale.

'Are you sure?'

'Yes,' said Mum. 'Take a look at him.'

Dad looked at Henry. Henry scowled.

'They're a *little* small, but not *that* bad,' said Dad.

'I can't breathe in these trousers!' shrieked Henry.

'That's why we're going shopping,'
said Mum. 'And *I'll* take him.' Last time
Dad had taken Henry shopping for
socks and came back instead with three
Hairy Hellhound CDs and a jumbo
pack of Day-Glo slime.

'I don't know what came over me,'
Dad had said, when Mum told him off.

'But why do *I* have to go?' said Henry.
'I don't want to waste my precious time
shopping.'

'What about *my* precious time?' said
Mum.

Henry scowled. Parents didn't have
precious time. They were there to serve
their children. New trousers should just
magically appear, like clean clothes and
packed lunches.

Mum's face brightened. 'Wait, I have
an idea,' she beamed. She rushed out
and came back with a large plastic bag.

'Here,' she said, pulling out
a pair of bright red
trousers, 'try these on.'

Henry looked at them
suspiciously.

'Where are they
from?'

'Aunt Ruby dropped
off some of Steve's old
clothes a few weeks ago. I'm
sure we'll find something that fits you.'

Horrid Henry stared at Mum. Had
she gone gaga? Was she actually
suggesting that he should wear his
horrible cousin's mouldy old shirts and
pongy pants? Just imagine, putting his
arms into the same stinky sleeves that
Stuck-up Steve had slimed? Uggh!

'NO WAY!' screamed Henry,
shuddering. 'I'm not wearing Steve's
smelly old clothes. I'd catch rabies.'

'They're practically brand new,' said Mum.

'I don't care,' said Henry.

'But Henry,' said Perfect Peter. 'I always wear *your* hand-me-downs.'

'So?' snarled Henry.

'I don't mind wearing hand-me-downs,' said Perfect Peter. 'It saves so much money. You shouldn't be so selfish, Henry.'

'Quite right, Peter,' said Mum, smiling. 'At least *one* of my sons thinks about others.'

Horrid Henry pounced. He was a vampire sampling his supper.

'AAIIIEEEEEE!' squealed Peter.

'Stop that, Henry!' screamed Mum.

'Leave your brother alone!' screamed Dad.

153

Horrid Henry glared at Peter.

'Peter is a worm, Peter is a toad,' jeered Henry.

'Mum!' wailed Peter. 'Henry said I was a worm. And a toad.'

'Don't be horrid, Henry,' said Dad. 'Or no TV for a week. You have three choices. Wear Steve's old clothes. Wear your old clothes. Go shopping for new ones today.'

'Do we *have* to go today?' moaned Henry.

'Fine,' said Mum. 'We'll go tomorrow.'

'I don't want to go tomorrow,' wailed Henry. 'My weekend will be ruined.'

Mum glared at Henry.

'Then we'll go right now this minute.'

'NO!' screamed Horrid Henry.

'YES!' screamed Mum.

★

Several hours later, Mum and Henry
walked into Mellow Mall. Mum already
looked like she'd been crossing the
Sahara desert
without water
for days. Serve
her right for
bringing me here,
thought Horrid
Henry, scowling,
as he scuffed his
feet.

'Can't we go
to Shop 'n'
Drop?' whined Henry. 'Graham says
they've got a win your weight in
chocolate competition.'

'No,' said Mum, dragging Henry into
Zippy's Department Store. 'We're here
to get you some new trousers and shoes.
Now hurry up, we don't have all day.'

Horrid Henry looked around. Wow! There was lots of great stuff on display.

'I want the Hip-Hop Robots,' said Henry.

'No,' said Mum.

'I want the new Supersoaker!' screeched Henry.

'No,' said Mum.

'I want a Creepy Crawly lunchbox!'

'NO!' said Mum, pulling him into the boys' clothing department.

What, thought Horrid Henry grimly, is the point of going shopping if you never buy anything?

'I want Root-a-Toot trainers with flashing red lights,' said Henry. He could see himself now, strolling into class, a bugle blasting and red light flashing every time his feet hit the floor. Cool! He'd love to see Miss Battle-Axe's face when he exploded into class wearing them.

'No,' said Mum, shuddering.

'Oh please,' said Henry.

'NO!' said Mum, 'we're here to buy trousers and sensible school shoes.'

'But I want Root-a-Toot trainers!' screamed Horrid Henry. 'Why can't we buy what *I* want to buy? You're the meanest mother in the world and I hate you!'

'Don't be horrid, Henry. Go and try these on,' said Mum, grabbing a selection of hideous trousers and revolting T-shirts. 'I'll keep looking.'

Horrid Henry sighed loudly and slumped towards the dressing room. No one in the world suffered as much as he did. Maybe he could hide between the clothes racks and never come out.

Then something wonderful in the toy department next door caught his eye.

Whooa! A whole row of the new megalotronic animobotic robots with 213 programmable actions. Horrid Henry dumped the clothes and ran over to have a look. Oooh, the new Intergalactic Samurai Gorillas which launched real stinkbombs! And the latest Supersoakers! And deluxe Dungeon Drink kits with a celebrity chef recipe book! To say nothing of the Mega-Whirl Goo Shooter which sprayed fluorescent goo for fifty metres in every direction. Wow!

Mum staggered into the dressing room with more clothes. 'Henry?' said Mum.

No reply.

'HENRY!' said Mum.

Still no reply.

Mum yanked open a dressing room door.

'Hen—'

'Excuse *me*!' yelped a bald man, standing in his underpants.

'Sorry,' said Mum, blushing bright pink. She dashed out of the changing room and scanned the shop floor.

Henry was gone.

Mum searched up the aisles.

No Henry.

Mum searched down the aisles.

Still no Henry.

Then Mum saw a tuft of hair sticking up behind the neon sign for Ballistic Bazooka Boomerangs. She marched over and hauled Henry away.

'I was just looking,' protested Henry.

Henry tried on one pair of trousers after another.

'No, no, no, no, no, no, no,' said Henry, kicking off the final pair. 'I hate all of them.'

'All right,' said Mum, grimly. 'We'll look somewhere else.'

Mum and Henry went to Top Trousers. They went to Cool Clothes. They went to Stomp in the Swamp. Nothing had been right.

'Too tight,' moaned Henry.

'Too itchy!'

'Too big!'

'Too small!'

'Too ugly!'

'Too red!'

'Too uncomfortable!'

'We're going to Tip-Top Togs,' said Mum wearily. 'The first thing that fits, we're buying.'

Mum staggered into the children's department and grabbed a pair of pink and green tartan trousers in Henry's size.

'Try these on,' she ordered. 'If they fit we're having them.'

Horrid Henry gazed in horror at the horrendous trousers.

'Those are girls' trousers!' he screamed.

'They are not,' said Mum.

'Are too!' shrieked Henry.

'I'm sick and tired of your excuses,

Henry,' said Mum. 'Put them on or no pocket money for a year. I mean it.'

Horrid Henry put on the pink and green tartan trousers, puffing out his stomach as much as possible. Not even Mum would make him buy trousers that were too tight.

Oh no. The horrible trousers had an elastic waist. They would fit a mouse as easily as an elephant.

'And lots of room to grow,' said Mum brightly. 'You can wear them for years. Perfect.'

'NOOOOOO!' howled Henry. He flung himself on the floor kicking and screaming. 'NOOOO! THEY'RE GIRLS' TROUSERS!!!'

'We're buying them,' said Mum. She gathered up the tartan trousers and stomped over to the till. She tried not to think about starting all over again trying to find a pair of shoes that Henry would wear.

A little girl in pigtails walked out of the dressing room, twirling in pink and green tartan trousers.

'I love them, Mummy!' she shrieked. 'Let's get three pairs.'

Horrid Henry stopped howling.

He looked at Mum.

Mum looked at Henry.

Then they both looked at the pink and green tartan trousers Mum was carrying.

ROOT-A-TOOT!
ROOT-A-TOOT!
ROOT-A-TOOT!
TOOT! TOOT!

An earsplitting bugle blast shook the house. Flashing red lights bounced off the walls.

'What's that noise?' said Dad, covering his ears.

'What noise?' said Mum, pretending to read.

ROOT-A-TOOT!
ROOT-A-TOOT!
ROOT-A-TOOT!
TOOT! TOOT!

Dad stared at Mum.

'You didn't,' said Dad. 'Not—Root-a-Toot trainers?'

Mum hid her face in her hands.

'I don't know what came over me,' said Mum.

HORRID HENRY'S ARCH ENEMY

'Be bop a lu la!' boomed Jazzy Jim, be-bopping round the class and bouncing to the beat.

'One day, my prince will come . . .' warbled Singing Soraya.

'Bam bam bam bam bam!' drummed Horrid Henry, crashing his books up and down on his table top.

'Class! Settle down!' shouted Miss Battle-Axe.

'Be bop a lu la!' boomed Jazzy Jim.

'One day, my prince will come . . .' warbled Singing Soraya.

'Bam bam bam bam bam!' drummed Horrid Henry.

'Jim!' barked Miss Battle-Axe. 'Stop yowling. Soraya! Stop singing. Henry! Stop banging or everyone will miss playtime.'

'Be bop—' faltered Jim.

'. . . prince will—' squeaked Soraya.

'Bam bam bam bam bam,' drummed Horrid Henry. He was Mad Moon Madison, crazy drummer for the

Mouldy Drumsticks, whipping the shrieking crowd into a frenzy—

'HENRY!' bellowed Miss Battle-Axe. 'STOP THAT NOISE!'

What did that ungrateful fan mean, noise? What noise? This wasn't noise, this was great music, this was—Mad Moon Madison looked up from his drum kit. Whoops.

Silence.

Miss Battle-Axe glared at her class. Oh, for the good old days, when

teachers could whack horrible children with rulers.

'Linda! Stop snoring. Graham! Stop drooling. Bert! Where's your chair?'

'I dunno,' said Beefy Bert.

There was a new boy standing next to

Miss Battle-Axe. His brown hair was tightly slicked back. His shoes were polished. He carried a trumpet and a calculator. Yuck! He looked like a complete idiot. Horrid Henry looked away. And then looked back. Funny, there was something familiar about that boy. The way he stood with his nose in the air. The horrid little smirk on his face. He looked like—he looked just like—oh no, please no, it couldn't be—Bossy Bill! Bossy Bill!!

'Class, we have a new boy,' said Miss Battle-Axe, doing her best to twist her thin lips into a welcoming smile. 'I need someone to look after him and show him around. Who would like to be Bill's friend for the day?'

Everyone put up their hand. Everyone but Horrid Henry. Uggh. Bossy Bill. What kind of cruel joke was this?

Bossy Bill was the horrible, stuck-up son of Dad's boss. Horrid Henry hated Bill. Uggh! Yuck! Just thinking about Bill made Henry gag.

Henry had a suspicion he wasn't Bill's favourite person, either. The last time they'd met, Henry had tricked Bill into photocopying his bottom. Bill had got into trouble. Big, big trouble.

Miss Battle-Axe scanned the sea of waving hands.

'Me!' shouted Moody Margaret.

'Me!' shouted Kind Kasim.

'Me!' shouted Weepy William.

'There's an empty seat next to Henry,' said Miss Battle-Axe, pointing. 'Henry will look after you.'

NO, thought Henry.

'Waaaaaa,' wailed Weepy William. 'I didn't get picked.'

'Go and sit down, Bill,' continued Miss Battle-Axe. 'Class, silent reading from page 12.'

Bossy Bill walked between the tables towards Horrid Henry.

Maybe he won't recognise me, thought Henry hopefully. After all, it was a long time ago.

Suddenly Bill stopped. His face contorted with loathing.

Oops.

He recognised me, thought Horrid Henry.

Bill marched, scowling, to the seat next to Henry and sat down. His nose wrinkled as if he smelled a stinky smell.

'You say one word about what happened at my dad's office and I'll tell my dad,' hissed Bill.

'You say one word to your dad and I'll tell everyone at school you photocopied

your bottom,' hissed Henry.

'Then I'll tell on you!'

'I'll tell on you!'

Bill shoved Henry.

Henry shoved Bill.

'He shoved me, miss!' shouted Bossy Bill.

'He shoved me first!' shouted Horrid Henry.

'Henry!' said Miss Battle-Axe. 'I am shocked and appalled. Is this how you welcome a new boy to our class?'

It is when the boy is Bossy Bill, thought Henry grimly.

He glared at Bill.

Bill glared at Henry.

'My old school's a lot better than this dump,' hissed Bossy Bill.

'So why don't you go back there?' hissed Henry. 'No one's stopping you.'

'Maybe I will,' said Bill.

Horrid Henry's heart leapt. Was there a chance he could get Bill to leave?

'You don't want to stay here—we get four hours of homework a night,' lied Henry.

'So?' said Bill. 'My old school gave you five hours.'

'The food's horrible.'

'Big deal,' said Bill.

'And Miss Battle-Axe is the meanest teacher in the world.'

'What did you say, Henry?' demanded Miss Battle-Axe's ice cold dagger voice.

'I just told Bill you were the keenest

teacher in the world,' said Henry quickly.

'No he didn't,' said Bill. 'He said you were the meanest.'

'Keenest,' said Henry.

'Meanest,' said Bill.

Miss Battle-Axe glared at Horrid Henry.

'I'm watching you, Henry. Now get back to work.'

DING! DING! DING!

Hurray! Saved by the playtime bell.

Horrid Henry jumped from his seat.
Maybe he could escape Bill if he ran
out of class fast enough.

Henry pushed and shoved his way
into the hall. Free! Free at last!

'Hey!' came an unwelcome voice
beside him. A sweaty hand pulled on his
shirt.

'The teacher said you're supposed to
show me around,' said Bossy Bill.

'OK, here are the toilets,' snarled
Horrid Henry, waving his hand in

the direction of the girls' loos. 'And
the photocopier's in the office,' he
added, pointing. 'Why don't you try
it out?'

Bill scowled.

'I'm going to tell my dad that you
attacked me,' said Bill. 'In fact, I'm going
to tell my dad every single bad thing
you do in school. Then he'll tell yours
and you'll get into trouble. And won't I
laugh.'

Henry's blood boiled. What had he
ever done to deserve Bossy Bill butting
into his life? A spy in his class. Could
school get any worse?

Aerobic Al jogged past.

'Henry photocopied his bottom at my
dad's office,' said Bill loudly. 'Boy, did he
get into trouble.'

AAARRRGGHHH!

'That's a lie,' said Horrid Henry hotly.

'Bill did, not me.'

'Yeah right, Henry,' said Dizzy Dave.

'Big bottom!' shrieked Moody
Margaret.

'Big big bottom!' shrieked Sour Susan.
Bill smirked.

'Bye, big bottom,' said Bill. 'Don't
forget, I'm watching you,' he hissed.

Henry sat down by himself on the
broken bench in the secret garden. He
had to get Bill out of his class. School
was horrible enough without someone

evil like Bill spying on him and
spreading foul rumours. His life would
be ruined. He had to get rid of Bill—
fast. But how?

Maybe he could get Bill to run
screaming from school and never come
back. Wow, thought Horrid Henry.
Wouldn't that be wonderful? Bye bye
Bossy Bill.

Or maybe he could get Bill to
photocopy his
bottom again.
Probably not,
thought Horrid
Henry
regretfully. Aha!
He could trick
Bill into dancing
nude on Miss
Battle-Axe's desk
singing 'I'm a busy

bumblebee—buzz buzz buzz.' That would be sure to get him expelled. The only trouble was—how?

I've got to think of something, thought Horrid Henry desperately. I've just got to.

'Henry,' said Dad the next evening, 'my boss tells me you've been picking on his son. Bill was very upset.'

'He's picking on *me*,' protested Henry.

'And that you were told off in class for shouting out.'

'No way,' lied Henry.

'And that you broke Andrew's pencil.'

'That was an accident,' said Henry.

'And that you called Margaret nitty-face.'

'I didn't,' wailed Henry. 'Bill's lying.'

'I want you to be on your best behaviour from now on,' said Dad. 'How do you think I feel hearing these reports about you from my boss? I've never been so embarrassed in my life.'

'Who cares?' screamed Horrid Henry. 'What about me?'

'Go to your room!' shouted Dad.

'FINE!' yelled Horrid Henry, slamming the door behind him as hard as he could. I'll beat you, Bill, thought Henry, if it's the last thing I do.

Horrid Henry tried teasing Bill. Horrid Henry tried pinching Bill. He tried spreading rumours about Bill. He even tried getting Bill to punch him so Bill would be suspended.

But nothing worked. Henry just got into more and more trouble.

On Monday Dad told Henry off for making rude noises in class.

On Tuesday Dad told Henry off for

talking during storytime.

On Wednesday Dad told Henry off for not handing in his homework.

On Thursday Mum and Dad yelled at Henry for chewing gum in class, passing notes to Ralph, throwing food, jiggling his desk, pulling Margaret's hair, running down the hall and kicking a football into the back playground. Then they banned him from the computer for a week. And all because of Bossy Bill.

★

Horrid Henry slunk into class. It was
hopeless. Bill was here to stay. Horrid
Henry would just have to grit his teeth
and bear it.

Miss Battle-Axe started explaining
electricity.

Henry looked around the classroom.
Speaking of Bill, where was he?

Maybe he has rabies, thought Horrid
Henry hopefully. Or fallen down the
toilet. Better still,
maybe he'd been
kidnapped by
aliens.

Or maybe
he'd been
expelled. Yes!
Henry could
see it now.
Bill on his

knees in Mrs Oddbod's office, begging to
stay. Mrs Oddbod pointing to the door:

'Out of this school, you horrible
monster! How dare you spy on Henry,
our best pupil?'

'NOOO!' Bill would wail.

'BEGONE, WRETCH!' commanded
Mrs Oddbod. And out went Bossy Bill,
snivelling, where armed
guards were waiting
to truss him up and
take him to prison.
That must be
what had happened.

Henry smiled.
Oh joyful day!
No more
Bossy Bill,
thought
Horrid
Henry

happily, stretching his legs under his
Bill-free table and taking a deep breath
of Bill-free air.

'Henry!' snapped Miss Battle-Axe.
'Come here.'

What now?

Slowly Horrid Henry heaved himself
out of his chair and scuffed his way to
Miss Battle-Axe's desk, where she was
busy slashing at homework with a
bright red pen.

'Bill has a sore throat,' said Miss Battle-Axe.

Rats, thought Horrid Henry. Where was the black plague when you needed it?

'His parents want him to have his homework assignments so he doesn't fall behind while he's ill,' said Miss Battle-Axe. 'If only *all* parents were so conscientious. Please give this maths worksheet to your father to give to Bill's dad.'

She handed Henry a piece of paper with ten multiplication sums on it and a large envelope.

'OK,' said Henry dully. Not even the thought of Bill lying in bed doing sums could cheer him up. All too soon Bill would be back. He was stuck with Bill for ever.

That night Horrid Henry glanced at

Bill's maths worksheet. Ten sums. Not enough, really, he thought. Why should Bill be bored in bed with nothing to do but watch TV, and read comics, and eat crisps?

And then Horrid Henry smiled. Bill wanted homework? Perhaps Henry could help. Tee hee, thought Horrid Henry, sitting down at the computer.

TAP

TAP

TAP

HOMEWERK

Rite a storee abowt yor day. 20 pages long.

Ha ha ha, that will keep Bill busy, thought Horrid Henry. Now, what else? What else?

Aha!

Give ten reesons why watching TV is better than reading

NEW MATHS

When does 2 + 2 =5 ?

When 2 is big enough.

Now explain why:

2+3=6

7-3=5

It was a lot more fun making up homework than doing it, thought Horrid Henry happily.

SPELLING:

Lern how to spel these words fer a test on Tuesday.

> **Terrantula**
> **Stinkbomb**
> **Moosli**
> **Doovay**
> **Screem**
> **Intergalactik**

SCEINSE

Gravity: does it work?

> **Drop an egg from a hight of 30 cm onto your mum or dad's hed.**

**_Record if it breaks. Drop
another egg from a hight
of 60 cm onto yor carpet.
Does this egg break? Try this xperiment
at least 12 times all over yor house._**

Now that's what I call homework,
thought Horrid Henry. He printed out
the worksheets, popped them in the
envelope with Miss
Battle-Axe's sheet of
sums, sealed it, and
gave it to Dad.

'Bill's homework,'
said Henry. 'Miss
Battle-Axe asked me
to give it to you to give to Bill's dad.'

'I'll make sure he gets it,' said Dad,
putting the envelope in his briefcase.
'I'm glad to see you're becoming friends
with Bill.'

Dad looked stern.

'I've got some bad news for you, Henry,' said Dad the next day.

Horrid Henry froze. What was he going to get told off about now? Oh no. Had Dad found out about what he'd done at lunchtime?

'I'm afraid Bill won't be coming back to your school,' said Dad. 'His parents have removed him. Something about new maths and a gravity experiment that went wrong.'

Horrid Henry's mouth opened. No

sound came out.

'Wha—?' gasped Horrid Henry.

'Gravity experiment?' said Mum. 'What gravity experiment?'

'Different science group,' said Henry quickly.

'Oh,' said Mum.

'Oh,' said Dad.

A lovely warm feeling spread from Henry's head all the way down to his toes.

'So Bill's not coming back?'

'No,' said Dad. 'I'm sorry that you've lost a friend.'

'I'll live,' beamed Horrid Henry.

Acknowledgements

Special thanks to Freddy Gaminara and Michael Garner for telling me so many exciting ways to cheat at football.

HORRID HENRY'S CHRISTMAS CRACKER

For the one and only
Miranda Richardson

CONTENTS

HORRiD HENRY'S CHRISTMAS PLAY

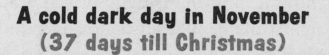

A cold dark day in November
(37 days till Christmas)

Horrid Henry slumped on the carpet and willed the clock to go faster. Only five more minutes to hometime! Already Henry could taste those crisps he'd be sneaking from the cupboard.

Miss Battle-Axe droned on about school dinners (yuck), the new drinking fountain blah blah blah, maths homework blah blah blah, the school Christmas play blah blah . . . what? Did Miss Battle-Axe say . . . Christmas play? Horrid Henry sat up.

'This is a brand-new play with singing and dancing,' continued Miss Battle-Axe. 'And both the older and the younger children are taking part this year.'

Singing! Dancing! Showing off in front of the whole school! Years ago, when Henry was in the infants' class, he'd played eighth sheep in the nativity play and had snatched the baby from the manger and refused to hand him back. Henry hoped Miss Battle-Axe wouldn't remember.

Because Henry had to play the lead. He had to. Who else but Henry could be an all-singing, all-dancing Joseph?

'I want to be Mary,' shouted every girl in the class.

'I want to be a wise man!' shouted Rude Ralph.

'I want to be a sheep!' shouted Anxious Andrew.

'I want to be Joseph!' shouted Horrid Henry.

'No, me!' shouted Jazzy Jim.

'Me!' shouted Brainy Brian.

'Quiet!' shrieked Miss Battle-Axe. 'I'm the director, and my decision about who will act which part is final. I've cast the play as follows: Margaret. You will be Mary.' She handed her a thick script.

Moody Margaret whooped with joy. All the other girls glared at her.

'Susan, front legs of the donkey; Linda, hind legs; cows, Fiona and Clare. Blades of grass—' Miss Battle-Axe continued assigning parts.

Pick me for Joseph, pick me for Joseph, Horrid Henry begged silently. Who better than the best actor in the school to play the starring part?

'I'm a sheep, I'm a sheep, I'm a

beautiful sheep!' warbled Singing Soraya.

'I'm a shepherd!' beamed Jolly Josh.

'I'm an angel,' trilled Magic Martha.

'I'm a blade of grass,' sobbed Weepy William.

'Joseph will be played by—'

'ME!' screamed Henry.

'Me!' screamed New Nick, Greedy Graham, Dizzy Dave and Aerobic Al.

'—Peter,' said Miss Battle-Axe. 'From Miss Lovely's class.'

Horrid Henry felt as if he'd been slugged in the stomach. Perfect Peter?

His *younger* brother? Perfect Peter get the starring part?

'It's not fair!' howled Horrid Henry.

Miss Battle-Axe glared at him.

'Henry, you're—' Miss Battle-Axe consulted her list. Please not a blade of grass, please not a blade of grass, prayed Horrid Henry, shrinking. That would be just like Miss Battle-Axe, to humiliate him. Anything but that—

'—the innkeeper.'

The innkeeper! Horrid Henry sat up, beaming. How stupid he'd been: the *innkeeper* must be the starring part. Henry could see himself now, polishing glasses, throwing darts, pouring out big foaming Fizzywizz drinks to all his happy customers while singing a song about the joys of innkeeping. Then he'd get into a nice long argument about why there was no room at the inn, and finally, the chance to slam the door in Moody

Margaret's face after he'd pushed her away.
Wow. Maybe he'd even get a second song.
'Ten Green Bottles' would fit right into
the story: he'd sing and dance while
knocking his less talented classmates off
a wall. Wouldn't that be fun!

Miss Battle-Axe handed a page to
Henry. 'Your script,' she said.

Henry was puzzled. Surely there were
some pages missing?

He read:

(Joseph knocks. The innkeeper opens the door.)

JOSEPH: Is there any room at the inn?
INNKEEPER: No.

(The innkeeper shuts the door.)

Horrid Henry turned over the page.

It was blank. He held it up to the light.

There was no secret writing. That was it.

His entire part was one line. One stupid puny line. Not even a line, a word. 'No.'

Where was his song? Where was his dance with the bottles and the guests at the inn? How could he, Horrid Henry, the best actor in the class (and indeed, the world) be given just one word in the school play? Even the donkeys got a song.

Worse, after he said his *one* word, Perfect Peter and Moody Margaret got to yack for hours about mangers and wise men and shepherds and sheep, and then sing a duet, while he, Henry, hung about behind the hay with the blades of grass.

It was so unfair!

He should be the star of the show, not his stupid worm of a brother. Why on earth was Peter cast as Joseph anyway? He was a terrible actor. He couldn't sing, he just squeaked like a squished toad. And why was Margaret playing Mary? Now she'd never stop bragging and swaggering.

AAARRRRGGGGHHHH!

'Isn't it exciting!' said Mum.

'Isn't it thrilling!' said Dad. 'Our little boy, the star of the show.'

'Well done, Peter,' said Mum.

'We're so proud of you,' said Dad.

Perfect Peter smiled modestly.

'Of course I'm not *really* the star,' he said, 'Everyone's important, even little parts like the blades of grass and the

innkeeper.'

Horrid Henry pounced. He was a Great White shark lunging for the kill.

'AAAARRRRGGGHH!' squealed Peter. 'Henry bit me!'

'Henry! Don't be horrid!' snapped Mum.

'Henry! Go to your room!' snapped Dad.

Horrid Henry stomped upstairs and

slammed the door. How could he bear
the humiliation of playing the innkeeper
when Peter was the star? He'd just have
to force Peter to switch roles with him.
Henry was sure he could find a way
to persuade Peter, but persuading Miss
Battle-Axe was a different matter. Miss
Battle-Axe had a mean, horrible way of
never doing what Henry wanted.

Maybe he could trick Peter into leaving
the show. Yes! And then nobly offer to
replace him.

But unfortunately, there was no
guarantee Miss Battle-Axe would give
Henry Peter's role. She'd probably just
replace Peter with Goody-Goody Gordon.
He was stuck.

And then Horrid Henry had a brilliant,
spectacular idea. Why hadn't he thought
of this before? If he couldn't play a bigger
part, he'd just have to make his part bigger.
For instance, he could *scream* 'No.' *That*

would get a reaction. Or he could bellow 'No,' and then hit Joseph. I'm an angry innkeeper, thought Horrid Henry, and I hate guests coming to my inn. Certainly smelly ones like Joseph. Or he could shout 'No!', hit Joseph, then rob him. I'm a robber innkeeper, thought Henry. Or, I'm a robber *pretending* to be an innkeeper. That would liven up the play a bit. Maybe he could be a French robber innkeeper, shout '*Non*', and rob Mary and Joseph. Or he was a French robber *pirate* innkeeper, so he could shout '*Non*,' tie Mary and Joseph up and make them walk the plank. Hmmm, thought Horrid Henry. Maybe my

part won't be so small. After all,
the innkeeper *was* the most important
character.

12 December
(only 13 more days till Christmas)

Rehearsals had been going on forever.
Horrid Henry spent most of his time
slumping in a chair. He'd never seen such
a boring play. Naturally he'd done everything he could to improve it.

'Can't I add a dance?' asked
Henry.

'No,' snapped Miss
Battle-Axe.

'Can't I add a
teeny-weeny-little
song?' Henry pleaded.

'No!' said Miss
Battle-Axe.

'But how does the

innkeeper *know* there's no room?' said
Henry. 'I think I should—'

Miss Battle-Axe glared at him with her
red eyes.

'One more word from you, Henry, and
you'll change places with Linda,' snapped
Miss Battle-Axe. 'Blades of grass, let's try
again . . .'

Eeek! An innkeeper with one word
was infinitely better than being invisible
as the hind legs of a donkey. Still—it was
so unfair. He was only trying to help.

22 December
(only 3 more days till Christmas!)

Showtime! Not a teatowel was to be
found in any local shop. Mums and dads
had been up all night frantically sewing
costumes. Now the waiting and the
rehearsing were over.

Everyone lined up on stage behind the

curtain. Peter and Margaret waited on the side to make their big entrance as Mary and Joseph.

'Isn't it exciting, Henry, being in a real play?' whispered Peter.

'NO,' snarled Henry.

'Places, everyone, for the opening song,' hissed Miss Battle-Axe. 'Now remember, don't worry if you make a little mistake: just carry on and no one will notice.'

'But I still think I should have an argument with Mary and Joseph about whether there's room,' said Henry. 'Shouldn't I at least check to see—'

'No!' snapped Miss Battle-Axe, glaring at him. 'If I hear another peep from you, Henry, you will sit behind the bales of hay and Jim will play your part. Blades of grass! Line up with the donkeys! Sheep! Get ready to baaa . . . Bert! Are you a sheep or a blade of grass?'

'I dunno,' said Beefy Bert.

Mrs Oddbod went to the front of the stage. 'Welcome everyone, mums and dads, boys and girls, to our new Christmas play, a little different from previous years. We hope you all enjoy a brand new show!'

Miss Battle-Axe started the CD player. The music pealed. The curtain rose. The audience stamped and cheered. Stars twinkled. Cows mooed. Horses neighed. Sheep baa'ed. Cameras flashed.

Horrid Henry stood in the wings and watched the shepherds do their Highland dance. He still hadn't decided for sure how he was going to play his part. There were so many possibilities. It was so hard to choose.

Finally, Henry's big moment arrived.

He strode across the stage and waited behind the closed inn door for Mary and Joseph.

Knock!

Knock!
Knock!

The innkeeper stepped forward and opened the door. There was Moody Margaret, simpering away as Mary, and Perfect Peter looking full of himself as Joseph.

'Is there any room at the inn?' asked Joseph.

Good question, thought Horrid Henry. His mind was blank. He'd thought of so many great things he *could* say that what he was *supposed* to say had just gone straight out of his head.

'Is there any room at the inn?' repeated Joseph loudly.

'Yes,' said the innkeeper. 'Come on in.'

Joseph looked at Mary.

Mary looked at Joseph.

The audience murmured.

Oops, thought Horrid Henry. Now he remembered. He'd been supposed to say no. Oh well, in for a penny, in for a pound.

The innkeeper grabbed Mary and Joseph's sleeves and yanked them through the door. 'Come on in, I haven't got all day.'

' . . . but . . . but . . . the inn's *full*,' said Mary.

'No it isn't,' said the innkeeper.

'Is too.'

'Is not. It's my inn and I should know. This is the best inn in Bethlehem, we've got TVs and beds, and—' the innkeeper paused for a moment. What *did* inns have in them? '—and computers!'

Mary glared at the innkeeper.

The innkeeper glared at Mary.

Miss Battle-Axe gestured frantically from the wings.

'This inn looks full to me,' said Mary firmly. 'Come on Joseph, let's go to the stable.'

'Oh, don't go there, you'll get fleas,' said the innkeeper.

'So?' said Mary.

'I love fleas,' said Joseph weakly.

'And it's full of manure.'

'So are you,' snapped Mary.

'Don't be horrid, Mary,' said the innkeeper severely. 'Now sit down and rest your weary bones and I'll sing you a song.' And the innkeeper started singing:

'Ten green bottles, standing on a wall
Ten green bottles, standing on a wall,
And if one green bottle should accidentally
  fall—'

'OOOHHH!' moaned Mary. 'I'm having the baby.'

'Can't you wait till I've finished my song?' snapped the inkeeper.

'NO!' bellowed Mary.

Miss Battle-Axe drew her hand across her throat.

Henry ignored her. After all, the show must go on.

'Come on, Joseph,' interrupted Mary. 'We're going to the stable.'

'OK,' said Joseph.

'You're making a big mistake,' said the innkeeper. 'We've got satellite TV and . . .'

Miss Battle-Axe ran on stage and nabbed him.

'Thank you, innkeeper, your other guests need you now,' said Miss Battle-Axe, grabbing him by the collar.

'Merry Christmas!' shrieked Horrid Henry as she yanked him off-stage.

There was a very long silence.

'Bravo!' yelled Moody Margaret's deaf aunt.

Mum and Dad weren't sure what to do. Should they clap, or run away to a place where no one knew them?

Mum clapped.

Dad hid his face in his hands.

'Do you think anyone noticed?' whispered Mum.

Dad looked at Mrs Oddbod's grim face. He sank down in his chair. Maybe one day he would learn how to make himself invisible.

'But what was I *supposed* to do?' said Horrid Henry afterwards in Mrs Oddbod's office. 'It's not *my* fault I forgot my line. Miss Battle-Axe said not to worry if we made a mistake and just to carry on.'

Could he help it if a star was born?

2

HORRID HENRY'S CHRISTMAS PRESENTS

23 December
(Just two more days to go!!!)

Horrid Henry sat by the Christmas tree and stuffed himself full of the special sweets he'd nicked from the special Christmas Day stash when Mum and Dad weren't looking. After his triumph in the school Christmas play, Horrid Henry was feeling delighted with himself and with the world.

Granny and Grandpa, his grown-up cousins Pimply Paul and Prissy Polly, and

their baby Vomiting Vera were coming
to spend Christmas. Whoopee, thought
Horrid Henry, because they'd all have
to bring *him* presents. Thankfully, Rich
Aunt Ruby and Stuck-Up Steve weren't
coming. They were off skiing. Henry
hadn't forgotten the dreadful lime green
cardigan Aunt Ruby had given him last
year. And much as he hated cousin Polly,
anyone was better than Stuck-Up Steve,
even someone who squealed all the
time and had a baby who threw up on
everyone.

Mum dashed into the sitting room,
wearing a flour-covered apron and
looking frantic. Henry choked down
his mouthful of sweets.

'Right, who wants to decorate the
tree?' said Mum. She held out a cardboard box brimming with tinsel and gold
and silver and blue baubles.

'Me!' said Henry.

'Me!' said Peter.

Horrid Henry dashed to the box and scooped up as many shiny ornaments as he could.

'I want to put on the gold baubles,' said Henry.

'I want to put on the tinsel,' said Peter.

'Keep away from my side of the tree,' hissed Henry.

'You don't have a side,' said Peter.

'Do too.'

'Do not,' said Peter.

'I want to put on the tinsel *and* the baubles,' said Henry.

'But I want to do the tinsel,' said Peter.

'Tough,' said Henry, draping Peter in tinsel.

'Muuum!' wailed Peter. 'Henry's hogging all the decorations! And he's putting tinsel on me.'

'Don't be horrid, Henry,' said Mum. 'Share with your brother.'

Peter carefully wrapped blue tinsel round the lower branches.

'Don't put it there,' said Henry, yanking it off. Trust Peter to ruin his beautiful plan.

'MUUUM!' wailed Peter.

'He's wrecking my design,' screeched Henry. 'He doesn't know how to decorate a tree.'

'But I wanted it there!' protested Peter. 'Leave my tinsel alone.'

'You leave my stuff alone then,' said Henry.

'He's wrecked my design!' shrieked Henry and Peter.

'Stop fighting, both of you!' shrieked
Mum.

'He started it!' screamed Henry.

'Did not!'

'Did too!'

'That's enough,' said Mum. 'Now,
whose turn is it to put the fairy on top?'

'I don't want to have that stupid fairy,'
wailed Horrid Henry. 'I want to have
Terminator Gladiator instead.'

'No,' said Peter. 'I want the fairy. We've
always had the fairy.'

'Terminator!'

'Fairy!'

'TERMINATOR!'

'FAIRY!'

Slap Slap

'WAAAAAAA!'

'We're having the fairy,' said Mum firmly, 'and *I'll* put it on the tree.'

'NOOOOOO!' screamed Henry. 'Why can't we do what I want to do? I never get to have what I want.'

'Liar!' whimpered Peter.

'I've had enough of this,' said Mum. 'Now get your presents and put them under the tree.'

Peter ran off.

Henry stood still.

'Henry,' said Mum. 'Have you finished wrapping your Christmas presents?'

Yikes, thought Horrid Henry. What am

I going to do now? The moment he'd
been dreading for weeks had arrived.

'Henry! I'm not going to ask you again,'
said Mum. 'Have you finished wrapping
all your Christmas presents?'

'Yes!' bellowed Horrid Henry.

This was not entirely true. Henry had
not finished wrapping his Christmas
presents. In fact, he hadn't even started.
The truth was, Henry had finished
wrapping because he had no presents to
wrap.

This was certainly *not* his fault. He *had*
bought a few gifts, certainly. He knew
Peter would love the box of green Day-
Glo slime. And if he didn't, well, he
knew who to give it to. And Granny and
Grandpa and Mum and Dad and Paul and
Polly would have adored the big boxes of
chocolates Henry had won at the school
fair. Could he help it if the chocolates
had called his name so loudly that he'd

been forced to eat them all? And then
Granny had been complaining about
gaining weight. Surely it would have
been very unkind to give her chocolate.
And eating chocolate would have just
made Pimply Paul's pimples worse.
Henry'd done him a big favour eating
that box.

And it was hardly Henry's fault when
he'd needed extra goo for a raid on the
Secret Club and Peter's present was the
only stuff to hand? He'd *meant* to buy
replacements. But he had so many things
he needed to buy for himself that when
he opened his skeleton bank to get out
some cash for Christmas shopping, only
35p had rolled out.

'I've bought and wrapped all *my*
presents, Mum,' said Perfect Peter. 'I've
been saving my pocket money for
months.'

'Whoopee for you,' said Henry.

'Henry, it's always better to give than to receive,' said Peter.

Mum beamed. 'Quite right, Peter.'

'Says who?' growled Horrid Henry. 'I'd much rather *get* presents.'

'Don't be so horrid, Henry,' said Mum.

'Don't be so selfish, Henry,' said Dad.

Horrid Henry stuck out his tongue. Mum and Dad gasped.

'You horrid boy,' said Mum.

'I just hope Father Christmas didn't see that,' said Dad.

'Henry,' said Peter, 'Father Christmas

won't bring you any presents if you're bad.'

AAARRRGGHHH! Horrid Henry sprang at Peter. He was a grizzly bear guzzling a juicy morsel.

'AAAAIIEEE,' wailed Peter. 'Henry pinched me.'

'Henry! Go to your room,' said Mum.

'Fine!' screamed Horrid Henry, stomping off and slamming the door. Why did he get stuck with the world's meanest and most horrible parents? *They* certainly didn't deserve any presents.

Presents! Why couldn't he just *get*

them? Why oh why did he have to *give* them? Giving other people presents was such a waste of his hard-earned money. Every time he gave a present it meant something he couldn't buy for himself. Goodbye chocolate. Goodbye comics. Goodbye Deluxe Goo-Shooter. And then, if you bought anything good, it was so horrible having to give it away. He'd practically cried having to give Ralph that Terminator Gladiator poster for his birthday. And the Mutant Max lunchbox Mum made him give Kasim still made him gnash his teeth whenever he saw Kasim with it.

Now he was stuck, on Christmas Eve, with no money, and no presents to give anyone, deserving or not.

And then Henry had a wonderful, spectacular idea. It was so wonderful, and so spectacular, that he couldn't believe he hadn't thought of it before.

Who said he had to *buy* presents? Didn't
Mum and Dad always say it was the
thought that counted? And oh boy was
he thinking.

Granny was sure to love a Mutant
Max comic. After all, who wouldn't?
Then when she'd finished enjoying it,
he could borrow it back. Horrid Henry
rummaged under his bed and found a
recent copy. In fact, it would be a shame
if Grandpa got jealous of Granny's great
present. Safer to give them each one,
thought Henry, digging deep into his
pile to find one with the fewest torn
pages.

Now let's see, Mum and Dad. He
could draw them a lovely picture. Nah,
that would take too long. Even better,
he could write them a poem.

Henry sat down at his desk, grabbed
a pencil, and wrote:

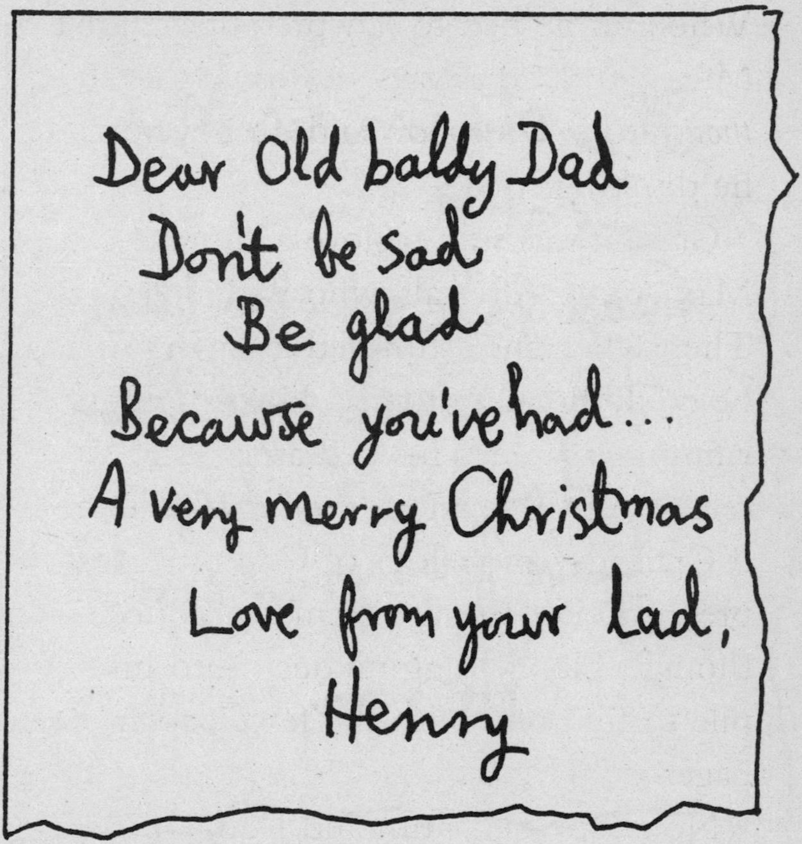

Dear Old baldy Dad
Don't be sad
Be glad
Because you've had...
A very merry Christmas
Love from your lad,
Henry

Not bad, thought Henry. Not bad. And so cheap! Now one for Mum.

Dear Old wrinkly Mum
Don't be glum
Cause you've got a fat tum
And an even bigger bum
Ho ho ho hum
Love from your son,

Henry

Wow! It was hard finding so many words to rhyme with *mum* but he'd done it. And the poem was nice and Christmasy with the 'ho ho ho'. *Son* didn't rhyme but hopefully Mum wouldn't notice

because she'd be so thrilled with the rest
of the poem. When he was famous she'd
be proud to show off the poem her son
had written specially for her.

Now, Polly. Hmmmn. She was always
squeaking and squealing
about dirt and dust. Maybe
a lovely kitchen sponge?
Or a rag she could use to
mop up after Vera? Or a
bucket to put over Pimply
Paul's head?

Wait. What about some
soap?

Horrid Henry nipped into the
bathroom. Yes! There was a tempting bar
of blue soap going to waste in the soap
dish by the bathtub. True, it had been used
once or twice, but a bit of smoothing with
his fingers would sort that out. In fact,
Polly and Paul could share this present,
it was such a good one.

Whistling, Horrid Henry wrapped up the soap in sparkling reindeer paper. He was a genius. Why hadn't he ever done this before? And a lovely rag from under the sink would be perfect as a gag for Vera.

That just left Peter and all his present problems would be over. A piece of chewing gum, only one careful owner? A collage of sweet wrappers which spelled out *Worm*? The unused comb Peter had given *him* last Christmas?

Aha. Peter loved bunnies. What better present than a picture of a bunny?

It was the work of a few moments for Henry to draw a bunny and slash a few blue lines across it to colour it in. Then he signed his name in big

letters at the bottom. Maybe he should be a famous artist and not a poet when he grew up, he thought, admiring his handiwork. Henry had heard that artists got paid loads of cash just for stacking a few bricks or hurling paint at a white canvas. Being an artist sounded like a great job, since it left so much time for playing computer games.

Horrid Henry dumped his presents beneath the Christmas tree and sighed happily. This was one Christmas where he was sure to get a lot more than he gave. Whoopee! Who could ask for anything more?

3

HORRID HENRY'S AMBUSH

Christmas Eve
(just a few more hours to go!)

It was Christmas Eve at last. Every minute felt like an hour. Every hour felt like a year. How could Henry live until Christmas morning when he could get his hands on all his loot?

Mum and Dad were baking frantically in the kitchen.

Perfect Peter sat by the twinkling Christmas tree scratching out 'Silent Night' over and over again on his cello.

'Can't you play something else?' snapped Henry.

'No,' said Peter, sawing away. 'This is the only Christmas carol I know. You can move if you don't like it.'

'You move,' said Henry.

Peter ignored him.

'Siiiiiiiii—lent Niiiiight,' screeched the cello.

AAARRRGH.

Horrid Henry lay on the sofa with his fingers in his ears, double-checking his choices from the Toy Heaven catalogue. Big red 'X's' appeared on every page, to help you-know-who remember all the toys he absolutely had to have. Oh please, let everything he wanted leap from its pages and into Santa's sack. After all, what could be better than looking at a huge glittering stack of presents on Christmas morning, and knowing that they were all for you?

Oh please let this be the year when he finally got everything he wanted!

His letter to Father Christmas couldn't have been clearer.

Dear Father Christmas,

I want loads and loads and loads of cash, to make up for the puny amount you put in my stocking last year. And a Robomatic Supersonic Space Howler Deluxe plus attachments would be great, too. I have asked for this before, you know!!! And the Terminator Gladiator fighting kit. I need lots more Day-Glo slime and comics and a Mutant Max poster and the new Zapatron Hip-Hop Dinosaur. This is your last chance.

Henry

PS. Satsumas are NOT presents!!!!!
PPS. Peter asked me to tell you to give me all his presents as he doesn't want any.

How hard could it be for Father Christmas to get this right? He'd asked for the Space Howler last year, and it never arrived. Instead, Henry got . . . vests. And handkerchiefs. And books. And clothes. And a—bleucccck—jigsaw puzzle and a skipping rope and a tiny supersoaker instead of the mega-sized one he'd specified. Yuck! Father Christmas obviously needed Henry's help.

Father Christmas is getting old and doddery, thought Henry. Maybe he hasn't got my letters. Maybe he's lost his reading glasses. Or—what a horrible thought—

maybe he was delivering Henry's presents by mistake to some other Henry. Eeeek! Some yucky, undeserving Henry was probably right now this minute playing with Henry's Terminator Gladiator sword, shield, axe, and trident. And enjoying his Intergalactic Samurai Gorillas. It was so unfair!

And then suddenly Henry had a brilliant, spectacular idea. Why had he never thought of this before? All his present problems would be over. Presents were far too important to leave to Father Christmas. Since he couldn't be trusted to bring the right gifts, Horrid Henry had no choice. He would have to ambush Father Christmas.

Yes!

He'd hold Father Christmas hostage with his Goo-Shooter, while he rummaged in his present sack for all the loot he was owed. Maybe Henry would keep the lot.

Now *that* would be fair.

Let's see, thought Horrid Henry. Father Christmas was bound to be a slippery character, so he'd need to booby-trap his bedroom. When you-know-who sneaked in to fill his stocking at the end of the bed, Henry could leap up and nab him. Father Christmas had a lot of explaining to do for all those years of stockings filled with satsumas and walnuts instead of chocolate and cold hard cash.

So, how best to capture him?

Henry considered.

A bucket of water above the door.

A skipping rope stretched tight across the entrance, guaranteed to trip up intruders.

A web of string criss-crossed from bedpost to door and threaded with bells to ensnare night-time visitors.

And let's not forget strategically scattered whoopee cushions.

His plan was foolproof.

Loot, here I come, thought Horrid
Henry.

Horrid Henry sat up in bed, his Goo-
Shooter aimed at the half-open door

where a bucket of water balanced. All his traps were laid. No one was getting in without Henry knowing about it. Any minute now, he'd catch Father Christmas and make him pay up.

Henry waited. And waited. And waited. His eyes started to feel heavy and he closed them for a moment.

There was a rustling at Henry's door.

Oh my god, this was it! Henry lay down and pretended to be asleep.

Cr-eeeek.

Cr-eeeek.

Horrid Henry reached for his Goo-Shooter.

A huge shape loomed in the doorway.

Henry braced himself to attack.

'Doesn't he look sweet when he's asleep?' whispered the shape.

'What a little snugglechops,' whispered another.

Sweet? Snugglechops?

Horrid Henry's fingers itched to let Mum and Dad have it with both barrels.

POW!

Splat!

Henry could see it now. Mum covered in green goo. Dad covered in green goo. Mum and Dad snatching the Goo-Shooter and wrecking all his plans and throwing

out all his presents and banning him from
TV for ever . . . hmmmn. His fingers felt
a little less itchy.

Henry lowered his Goo-Shooter. The
bucket of water wobbled above the door.

Yikes! What if Mum and Dad stepped
into his Santa traps? All his hard work—
ruined.

'I'm awake,' snarled Henry.

The shapes stepped back. The water
stopped wobbling.

'Go to sleep!' hissed Mum.

'Go to sleep!' hissed Dad.

'What are you doing here?' demanded
Henry.

'Checking on you,' said Mum. 'Now go
to sleep or Father Christmas will never
come.'

He'd better, thought Henry.

Horrid Henry woke with a jolt.
AAARRGGH! He'd fallen asleep. How

could he? Panting and gasping Henry switched on the light. Phew. His traps were intact. His stocking was empty. Father Christmas hadn't been yet.

Wow, was that lucky. That was incredibly lucky. Henry lay back, his heart pounding.

And then Horrid Henry had a terrible thought.

What if Father Christmas had decided to be spiteful and *avoid* Henry's bedroom this year? Or what if he'd played a sneaky trick on Henry and filled a stocking *downstairs* instead?

Nah. No way.

But wait. When Father Christmas came to Rude Ralph's house he always filled the stockings downstairs. Now Henry came to think of it, Moody Margaret always left her stocking downstairs too, hanging from the fireplace, not from the end of her bed, like Henry did.

Horrid Henry looked at the clock. It

was past midnight. Mum and Dad had forbidden him to go downstairs till morning, on pain of having all his presents taken away and no telly all day.

But this was an emergency. He'd creep downstairs, take a quick peek to make sure he hadn't missed Father Christmas, then be back in bed in a jiffy.

No one will ever know, thought Horrid Henry.

Henry tiptoed round the whoopee cushions, leaped over the criss-cross threads, stepped over the skipping rope and carefully squeezed through his door so as not to disturb the bucket of water. Then he crept downstairs.

Sneak
   Sneak
      Sneak

Horrid Henry shone his torch over the sitting room. Father Christmas hadn't been. The room was exactly as he'd left it that evening.

Except for one thing. Henry's light illuminated the Christmas tree, heavy with chocolate santas and chocolate bells and chocolate reindeer. Mum and Dad must have hung them on the tree after he'd gone to bed.

Horrid Henry looked at the chocolates cluttering up the Christmas tree. Shame, thought Horrid Henry, the way those chocolates spoil the view of all those lovely decorations. You could barely see the baubles and tinsel he and Peter had worked so hard to put on.

'Hi, Henry,' said the chocolate santas. 'Don't you want to eat us?'

'Go on, Henry,' said the chocolate bells.

'You know you want to.'

'What are you waiting for, Henry?' urged the chocolate reindeer.

What indeed? After all, it *was* Christmas.

Henry took a chocolate santa or three from the side, and then another two from the back. Hmmn, boy, was that great chocolate, he thought, stuffing them into his mouth.

Oops. Now the chocolate santas looked a little unbalanced.

Better take a few from the front and from the other side, to even it up, thought Henry. Then no one will notice there are a few chocolates missing.

Henry gobbled and gorged and guzzled. Wow, were those chocolates yummy!!!

The tree looks a bit bare, thought Henry a little while later. Mum had such eagle eyes she might notice that a few— well, all—of the chocolates were missing. He'd better hide all those gaps with a

few extra baubles. And, while he was
improving the tree, he could swap that
stupid fairy for Terminator Gladiator.

Henry piled extra decorations onto the
branches. Soon the Christmas tree was
so covered in baubles and tinsel there
was barely a hint of green. No one
would notice the missing chocolates.
Then Henry stood on a chair, dumped
the fairy, and, standing on his tippy-tippy
toes, hung Terminator Gladiator at the
top where he belonged.

Perfect, thought Horrid Henry, jumping off the chair and stepping back to admire his work. Absolutely perfect. Thanks to me this is the best tree ever.

There was a terrible creaking sound. Then another. Then suddenly . . .

CRASH!

The Christmas tree toppled over.

Horrid Henry's heart stopped.

Upstairs he could hear Mum and Dad stirring.

'Oy! Who's down there?' shouted Dad.

RUN!!! thought Horrid Henry. Run for your life!!

Horrid Henry ran like he had never run before, up the stairs to his room before Mum and Dad could catch him. Oh please let him get there in time. His parents' bedroom door opened just as Henry dashed inside his room. He'd made it. He was safe.

SPLASH! The bucket of water spilled all over him.

TRIP! Horrid Henry fell over the skipping rope.

CRASH! SMASH!

RING! RING! jangled the bells.

PLLLLLLL! belched the whoopee cushions.

'What is going on in here?' shrieked Mum, glaring.

'Nothing,' said Horrid Henry, as he lay sprawled on the floor soaking wet and tangled up in threads and wires and rope. 'I heard a noise downstairs so I got up to check,' he added innocently.

'Tree's fallen over,' called Dad. 'Must have been overloaded. Don't worry, I'll sort it.'

'Get back to bed, Henry,' said Mum wearily. 'And don't touch your stocking till morning.'

Henry looked. And gasped. His stocking was stuffed and bulging. That mean old sneak, thought Horrid Henry indignantly. How did he do it? How had he escaped the traps?

Watch out Father Christmas, thought Horrid Henry. I'll get you next year.

HORRiD HENRY'S CHRISTMAS LUNCH

25 December (at last!)

'Oh, handkerchiefs, just what I wanted,' said Perfect Peter. 'Thank you *so* much.'

'Not handkerchiefs *again*,' moaned Horrid Henry, throwing the hankies aside and ripping the paper off the next present in his pile.

'Don't tear the wrapping paper!' squeaked Perfect Peter.

Horrid Henry ripped open the present and groaned.

Yuck (a pen, pencil, and ruler). Yuck (a dictionary). Yuck (gloves). OK (£15—should have been a lot more). Eeew (a pink bow tie from Aunt Ruby). Eeew (mints). Yum (huge tin of chocolates). Good (five more knights for his army). Very good (a subscription to Gross-Out Fan Club) . . .

And (very very good) a Terminator Gladiator trident . . . and . . .

And . . . where was the rest?

'Is that it?' shrieked Henry.

'You haven't opened my present, Henry,' said Peter. 'I hope you like it.'

Horrid Henry tore off the wrapping. It was a Manners With Maggie calendar.

'Ugh, gross,' said Henry. 'No thank you.'

'Henry!' said Mum. 'That's no way to receive a present.'

'I don't care,' moaned Horrid Henry. 'Where's my Zapatron Hip-Hop

dinosaur? And where's the rest of the
Terminator Gladiator fighting kit? I
wanted everything, not just the trident.'

'Maybe next year,' said Mum.

'But I want it now!' howled Henry.

'Henry, you know that "I want doesn't
get",' said Peter. 'Isn't that right, Mum?'

'It certainly is,' said Mum. 'And I
haven't heard you say thank you, Henry.'

Horrid Henry glared at Peter and
sprang. He was a hornet stinging a worm
to death.

'WAAAAAAH!' wailed Peter.

'Henry! Stop it or—'

Ding! Dong!

'They're here!' shouted Horrid Henry, leaping up and abandoning his prey. 'That means more presents!'

'Wait, Henry,' said Mum.

But too late. Henry raced to the door and flung it open.

There stood Granny and Grandpa, Prissy Polly, Pimply Paul, and Vomiting Vera.

'Gimme my presents!' he shrieked, snatching a bag of brightly wrapped gifts out of Granny's hand and spilling them on the floor. Now, where were the ones with his name on?

'Merry Christmas, everyone,' said Mum brightly. 'Henry, don't be rude.'

'I'm not being rude,' said Henry. 'I just

want my presents. Great, money!' said
Henry, beaming. 'Thanks, Granny! But
couldn't you add a few pounds and—'

'Henry, don't be horrid!' snapped Dad.

'Let the guests take off their coats,' said
Mum.

'Bleeeeech,' said Vomiting Vera, throwing
up on Paul.

'Eeeeek,' said Polly.

All the grown-ups gathered in the sitting
room to open their gifts.

'Peter, thank you so much for the
perfume, it's my favourite,' said Granny.

'I know,' said Peter.

'And what a lovely comic, Henry,' said Granny. 'Mutant Max is my . . . um . . . favourite.'

'Thank you, Henry,' said Grandpa. 'This comic looks very . . . interesting.'

'I'll have it back when you've finished with it,' said Henry.

'Henry!' said Mum, glaring.

For some reason Polly didn't look delighted with her present.

'Eeeek!' squeaked Polly. 'This soap has . . . hairs in it.' She pulled out a long black one.

'That came

free,' said Horrid Henry.

'We're getting you toothpaste next year, you little brat,' muttered Pimply Paul under his breath.

Honestly, there was no pleasing some people, thought Horrid Henry indignantly. He'd given Paul a great bar of soap, and he didn't seem thrilled. So much for it's the thought that counts.

'A poem,' said Mum. 'Henry, how lovely.'

'Read it out loud,' said Grandpa.

'Dear old wrinkly Mum
Don't be glum
'Cause you've got a fat tum
And an even bigger...'

'Maybe later,' said Mum.

'Another poem,' said Dad. 'Great!'

'Let's hear it,' said Granny.

'Dear old baldy Dad—

. . . and so forth,' said Dad, folding Henry's poem quickly.

'Oh,' said Polly, staring at the crystal frog vase Mum and Dad had given her.

'How funny. This looks just like the vase *I* gave Aunt Ruby for Christmas last year.'

'What a coincidence,' said Mum, blushing bright red.

'Great minds think alike,' said Dad quickly.

Dad gave Mum an iron.

'Oh, an iron, just what
I always wanted,'
said Mum.

Mum gave Dad
oven gloves.

'Oh, oven gloves,
just what I always
wanted,' said Dad.

Pimply Paul
gave Prissy Polly a
huge power drill.
'Eeeek,' squealed
Polly. 'What's this?'
'Oh, that's the
Megawatt Superduper
Drill-o-matic 670
XM3,' said Paul, 'and just wait till you see
the attachments. You're getting those for
your birthday.'

'Oh,' said Polly.

Granny gave Grandpa a lovely mug to put his false teeth in.

Grandpa gave Granny a shower cap and a bumper pack of dusters.

'What super presents!' said Mum.

'Yes,' said Perfect Peter. 'I loved every single one of my presents, especially the satsumas and walnuts in my stocking.'

'I didn't,' said Horrid Henry.

'Henry, don't be horrid,' said Dad. 'Who'd like a mince pie?'

'Are they homemade or from the shop?' asked Henry.

'Homemade of course,' said Dad.

'Gross,' said Henry.

'Ooh,' said Polly. 'No, Vera!' she squealed as Vera vomited all over the plate.

'Never mind,' said Mum tightly. 'There's more in the kitchen.'

Horrid Henry was bored. Horrid Henry was fed up. The presents had all been opened. His parents had made him go on a long, boring walk. Dad had confiscated his Terminator trident when he had speared Peter with it.

So, what now?

Grandpa was sitting in the armchair with his pipe, snoring, his tinsel crown slipping over his face.

Prissy Polly and Pimply Paul were squabbling over whose turn it was to change Vera's stinky nappy.

'Eeeek,' said Polly. 'I did it last.'

'I did,' said Paul.

'WAAAAAAAAA!' wailed Vomiting Vera.

Perfect Peter was watching Sammy the Snail slithering about on TV.

Horrid Henry snatched the clicker and switched channels.

'Hey, I was watching that!' protested Peter.

'Tough,' said Henry.

Let's see, what was on? 'Tra la la la . . .' Ick! Daffy and her Dancing Daisies.

'Wait! I want to watch!' wailed Peter.

Click.' . . . and the tension builds as the judges compare tomatoes grown . . .' Click! ' . . . wish you a Merry Christmas, we wish you . . .' Click! 'Chartres Cathedral is one of the wonders of . . .' Click! 'HA HA HA HA HA HA HA HA.' Opera! Click! Why was there nothing good on TV? Just a baby movie about singing cars he'd seen a million times already.

'I'm bored,' moaned Henry. 'And I'm starving.' He wandered into the kitchen, which looked like a hurricane had swept through.

'When's lunch? I thought we were eating at two. I'm starving.'

'Soon,' said Mum. She looked a little

frazzled. 'There's been a little problem with the oven.'

'So when's lunch?' bellowed Horrid Henry.

'When it's ready!' bellowed Dad.

Henry waited. And waited. And waited.

'When's lunch?' asked Polly.

'When's lunch?' asked Paul.

'When's lunch?' asked Peter.

'As soon as the turkey is cooked,' said Dad. He peeked into the oven. He poked the turkey. Then he went pale.

'It's hardly cooked,' he whispered.

'Check the temperature,' said Granny.

Dad checked.

'Oops,' said Dad.

'Never mind, we can start with the sprouts,' said Mum cheerfully.

'That's not the right way to do sprouts,' said Granny. 'You're peeling too many of the leaves off.'

'Yes, Mother,' said Dad.

'That's not the right way to make bread sauce,' said Granny.

'Yes, Mother,' said Dad.

'That's not the right way to make stuffing,' said Granny.

'Yes, Mother,' said Dad.

'That's not the right way to roast potatoes,' said Granny.

'Mother!' yelped Dad. 'Leave me alone!'

'Don't be horrid,' said Granny.

'I'm not being horrid,' said Dad.

'Come along Granny, let's get you a nice drink and leave the chef on his own,' said Mum, steering Granny firmly towards the sitting room. Then she stopped.

'Is something burning?' asked Mum, sniffing.

Dad checked the oven.

'Not in here.'

There was a shriek from the sitting room.

'It's Grandpa!' shouted Perfect Peter.

Everyone ran in.

There was Grandpa, asleep in his chair. A thin column of black smoke rose from

the arms. His paper crown, drooping over
his pipe, was smoking.

'Whh..whh?' mumbled Grandpa, as
Mum whacked him with her broom.
'AAARRGH!' he gurgled as Dad threw
water over him.

'When's lunch?' screamed Horrid
Henry.

'When it's ready,' screamed Dad.

★

It was dark when Henry's family finally sat down to Christmas lunch. Henry's tummy was rumbling so loudly with hunger he thought the walls would cave in. Henry and Peter made a dash to grab the seat against the wall, furthest from the kitchen.

'Get off!' shouted Henry.

'It's my turn to sit here,' wailed Peter.

'Mine!'

'Mine!'

Slap!

Slap!

'WAAAAAAAAAAA!' screeched Henry.

'WAAAAAAAAAAA!' wailed Peter.

'Quiet!' screamed Dad.

Mum brought in fresh holly and ivy to decorate the table.

'Lovely,' said Mum, placing the boughs all along the centre.

'Very festive,' said Granny.

'I'm starving!' wailed Horrid Henry.
'This isn't Christmas lunch, it's Christmas
dinner.'

'Shhh,' said Grandpa.

The turkey was finally cooked. There
were platefuls of stuffing, sprouts,
cranberries, bread sauce and peas.

'Smells good,' said Granny.

'Hmmn, boy,' said Grandpa. 'What a feast.'

Horrid Henry was so hungry he could eat the tablecloth.

'Come on, let's eat!' he said.

'Hold on, I'll just get the roast potatoes,' said Dad. Wearing his new oven gloves, he carried in the steaming hot potatoes in a glass roasting dish, and set it in the middle of the table.

'*Voila!*' said Dad. 'Now, who wants dark meat and who . . .'

'What's that crawling . . . aaaarrrghh!' screamed Polly. 'There are spiders every-where!'

282

Millions of tiny
spiders were pouring from
the holly and crawling
all over the table and
the food.

'Don't panic!'
shouted Pimply Paul,
leaping from his
chair, 'I know
what to do, we
just—'

But before
he could do
anything the glass dish with the roast
potatoes exploded.

CRASH!

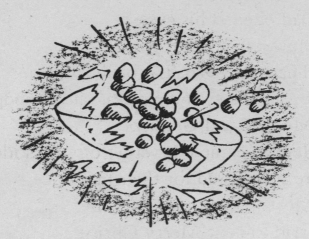

SMASH!

'EEEEEKK!' screamed Polly.

Everyone stared at the slivers of glass glistening all over the table and the food.

Dad sank down in his chair and covered his eyes.

'Where are we going to get more food?' whispered Mum.

'I don't know,' muttered Dad.

'I know,' said Horrid Henry, 'let's start with Christmas pudding and defrost some pizzas.'

Dad opened his eyes.

Mum opened her eyes.

'That,' said Dad, 'is a brilliant idea.'

'I really fancy some pizza,' said Grandpa.

'Me too,' said Granny.

Henry beamed. It wasn't often his ideas were recognised for their brilliance.

'Merry Christmas everyone,' said Horrid Henry. 'Merry Christmas.'

Acknowledgements

My thanks to Susie Boyt, Amanda
Craig, Judith Elliott, Fiona Kennedy
and Kate Saunders for sharing their
Christmas disaster stories
with me.

The HORRID HENRY books
by Francesca Simon

Illustrated by Tony Ross

Each book contains four stories

HORRID HENRY

Henry is dragged to dancing class against his will; vies with Moody Margaret to make the yuckiest Glop, goes camping in France and tries to be good like Perfect Peter – but not for long.

HORRID HENRY

AND THE SECRET CLUB

Horrid Henry gets an injection, torments
his little brother Perfect Peter, creates
havoc at his own birthday party, and plans
sweet revenge when Moody Margaret
won't let him into her Secret Club.

HORRID HENRY
TRICKS THE TOOTH FAIRY

(Originally published as
Horrid Henry and the Tooth Fairy)

Horrid Henry tries to trick the Tooth
Fairy into giving him more money, sends
Moody Margaret packing, causes his
teachers to run screaming from school,
and single-handedly wrecks a wedding.

HORRID HENRY'S
NITS

Scratch. Scratch. Scratch. Horrid Henry has nits – and he's on a mission to give them to everyone else too. After that, he can turn his attention to wrecking the school trip, ruining his parents' dinner party, and terrifying Perfect Peter.

HORRID HENRY'S
HAUNTED HOUSE

Horrid Henry slugs it out with Perfect
Peter over the remote control, stays in a
haunted house and gets a nasty shock,
discovers where X marks the spot in
the hidden treasure competition and
stars on TV.

HORRID HENRY
GETS RICH QUICK

(Originally published as
Horrid Henry Strikes It Rich)

Horrid Henry tries to sell off Perfect
Peter and get rich, makes sure he gets
the presents he wants for Christmas,
sabotages Sports Day at school – and
runs away from home.

HORRID HENRY

is also available on audio cassette and CD,
all read by Miranda Richardson

'A hoot from beginning to end ... As always,
Miranda Richardson's delivery is perfection and
the manic music is a delight.' *Daily Express*

'Long may this dreadful boy continue to
terrorise all who know him. He's a nightmare,
but so entertaining ...' *Parents' Guide*